Also by Pauline Chandler

WARRIOR GIRL

'A terrific tale set in medieval France.
When Mariane's parents are murdered, she's drawn to her
strange cousin, Jehanne, who claims she gets signs
from God. You'll be left breathless with pure excitement.'
Mizz magazine

'the healing revelation with which this novel
ends is so unexpected and utterly right
that it made me gulp'
Kevin Crossley-Holland, writing in the *Guardian*

VIKING GIRL

PAULINE CHANDLER

OXFORD
UNIVERSITY PRESS

OXFORD

UNIVERSITY PRESS

Great Clarendon Street, Oxford OX2 6DP

Oxford University Press is a department of the University of Oxford.
It furthers the University's objective of excellence in research, scholarship,
and education by publishing worldwide in

Oxford   New York

Auckland   Cape Town   Dar es Salaam   Hong Kong   Karachi
Kuala Lumpur   Madrid   Melbourne   Mexico City   Nairobi
New Delhi   Shanghai   Taipei   Toronto

With offices in

Argentina   Austria   Brazil   Chile   Czech Republic   France   Greece
Guatemala   Hungary   Italy   Japan   Poland   Portugal   Singapore
South Korea   Switzerland   Thailand   Turkey   Ukraine   Vietnam

Oxford is a registered trade mark of Oxford University Press
in the UK and in certain other countries

British Library Cataloguing in Publication Data

Data available

ISBN: 978-0-19-275497-4

1 3 5 7 9 10 8 6 4 2

Printed in Great Britain by Cox and Wyman Ltd, Reading, Berkshire

For Si, Matt, and Ben

CONTENTS

CHAPTER 1
HUNTING

The nights seem darker here. I expect it's the trees; this Eng-land, from what I've seen of it, is thick with woods. Back home in the Mark, I could always see clear to the horizon in all directions, and spot an enemy from a thousand paces. Here I skulk as a thief in the twilight, hiding, forever hiding, ears pricked for the hiss of a Saxon dart.

I stumbled down a rough track, leaving the river behind, moving deeper into Saxon territory, and my hawk Raed stirred, restless, on my shoulder. *Tss . . . tss . . . there . . .* I stroked Raed's feathers to calm her.

I risk much hunting on the Saxon side of the river, but I have no choice: there's game here, I've seen it on previous forays—pigeon, snake, stoat—meagre enough, but better than nothing. My people are starving and I am their leader. What sort of leader am I if I cannot even feed my own people?

I burst into a clearing, took Raed from my shoulder, and held her high on my wrist. She stretched herself ready to fly, first one wing then the other, flexing her long yellow claws, digging them deep into the leather guard on my arm. *'Sharp beak . . . Clear eye . . . Clean kill,'* I whispered, pressing my lips close to her neck, then I jerked my arm and sent her into the sky. *'Good hunting, stormrider,'* I murmured, as I settled back on my haunches to watch my Viking hawk quarter the Saxon wood.

Let me explain the lie of the land. The place we came to, where we made our camp, is near the coast, to the east of the river. It is bounded on three sides by water. East is the sea, north and west the river, holding us in a curving embrace. South, after a long stretch of woods— a day's march—there is marshland, dangerous territory, where you could sink into the bog and be lost within a breath. In the first weeks we took fish from the river and from the sea, but not enough. When I needed to hunt further for meat, I crossed the river to where the Saxons were.

As queen of my tribe, I should show myself openly to our old enemies, I should talk to them, now that the long war between Saxons and Vikings for rule over all Eng-land is almost at an end. In the north Halfdan has established his court at Jorvik. In the south, Lord Guthrum is on the point of victory against the Saxon King Aelfred. There will be peace.

But how do we make friends with those we have conquered? How do we live together? From what I have seen, the Saxons hate us, so I must be cautious: the lives of my people depend on it. We are a small band—thirty-two souls—and a long way from our nearest allies: if the Saxons chose, they could wipe us out before Halfdan's men come to our aid. My band is too weak to take what we need by force: we must trade for it or turn thief.

How I hate all this skulking. Nightstalker. That's what I've become. Shadow-walker. Robberwraith. It is not who I am.

I was Berengeria, daughter of Thorkil, king of the Mark. Now I am a queen with no land, an exile with a handful of warriors, forced into hiding.

I took a risk, on the day we arrived, stayed out in the open to build the home shelter, using a bright sail for the roof—the red and white stripes might have attracted the Saxons' attention—but after trudging our way from the sea, hefting our few possessions like a line of old beggars, we needed a soul-easing, so I gave the order to use the sail.

Grymma and Tyr, the oldest warriors, argued caution, but it was the right decision. I knew that when Helga, sail-maker, started to sing. Laying hold on the sail, she threw it open and she started to sing, as if she were back in the yard at home, calling the men in for their dinner. She sang the one about old Tostig and Etta the milkmaid. Do you know it? Saxons or no Saxons, we all rocked with the song as we spread the sail, singing all verses, every last one.

We made such a din as we worked, bending the branches of saplings and shoving them into the dark earth, as if we'd made a shelter like this a thousand times before. We gave a shout to shake the very gods themselves in the goldhalls of Asgard, as we chucked the sail over the framework, as if we were launching a new ship. Ha. That was a feeling. Brokk the smith complaining as usual when he had to find more stones to hold down the sail. Brand, my hearth companion, and his brother Leif Ropemaker, stern-faced, drawing swords to stand on guard, though there was no sign of the Saxons, like the old ones watching over a party of children. Sigrid Ulfsdatter clearing a place for the hearthfire, warming the last of the ale and making us all have a taste, even little Gerd.

Asa, my loved stepmother, in all places at once, herding her flock, no longer of sheep—she left those behind in the Mark. Skar settling the hawks. And I—giving orders as if I had been queen forever, not just for a few days.

There we dropped anchor, deep in the Saxon woods, five hundred paces, no more, from the sea, and it was worth the risk of alerting the Saxons, because in working together, we found a way to safe harbour, a way to make home again.

Saxons or no, we determined to stay, and there we marked out our steading. I and my people, my tribe, my poor remnant, defeated in the last battle for the Mark, driven into exile, into an alien land. I prayed to Great God Othinn, often and long, to protect us.

My belly aches. Why did I not take the stale bannock Asa offered to me as I left the shelter?

I shifted my buttocks, the wet hide of my breeks chafing the wound on my leg, so that I squirmed like an adder. I was glad it was almost healed; things could have been worse: Great Othinn had smiled on me. I uttered another prayer: *send me food . . .*

That was a bitter day when we fought our last battle for the Mark. The wind and the enemy came from the east, both blasting us back, ever back to the sea. The Jutlanders came upon us thousand fold, like ravening wolves. I fought with sword and axe, hacking through flesh and bone, feeling the hot blood spurt on my own flesh; I wiped one man's blood from my eyes—whenever the nightmare rode me I could still feel it—and I lost count of my enemies' deaths. I still saw my father's flag, the banner of Thorkil the king, its red fox flying out; I saw the flash of his silver horn as again and again he sounded 'Attack! Attack!' I felt the blood-shock again, when I knew that we would fail.

As the fight swung towards me, my companions—Brand, Brokk, Helga, Skar—stood at my side. It was not enough. Too soon the cry went up that my father, Thorkil, the king, had been killed. We had our backs to the sea and even the crashing tide seemed against us. Rocked by the waves, thigh-deep, I lowered my weapons and the others copied my gesture. None continued the fight, once I had lowered my sword, because, when Thorkil died, was when I became queen.

On the eve of battle, my father took the golden crown from his head and passed it to me, asking the jarl-companions to bear *witness*, that I, his daughter, Beren, should be queen, if he was killed on the field. I was surprised. Why did the crown not pass to my father-brother, my uncle Vasser? Vasser might have expected it. He was a strong warrior and, though harsh, a respected leader. He seemed shocked by Thorkil's bequest: I saw his sour stretched smile, as Thorkil held out the crown to me. *Why me and not Vasser?* That thought didn't last the next swill of ale: as the cheers sounded out and I took the crown, kissed it, then passed it quickly back to my father, my head filled with dreams of gold thrones and treasure. Of course I did not think that my father would die. Nevertheless, I was made formally his heir, something I had not expected. I had no proper understanding of what it meant to be queen. I had no real idea of what it meant. I was a child.

Only then, on the field, when I lowered my sword and the rest followed, then, with a rush of knowledge, as if from the High God Othinn himself, I understood it. To be queen meant that whatever I asked of them, my people would obey. Wherever I went they would follow; they had put their lives in my hands. I had become their friend and protector. It was my task to fight for them, shelter them, rule them, and feed them. I was queen.

My uncle Vasser soon came to me, pushing his way through the living and the dead. Like a newly born foal, I was struggling to find my balance, and in that first hour of weakness, Vasser took charge—he was careful to inform me of every step that he took—but it was Vasser who bargained with the enemy to gain our freedom.

Under enemy eyes, I gathered myself, washed my sword and axe clean and shoved them back in my belt. Then I cleaned the blood from my hands, dashed salt water over my face, and took note of my people. Asa,

Thorkil's wife, my stepmother, had gathered them into groups on the strand. Worn, bedraggled, blood-spattered, they were pitifully few. I was queen of a remnant only.

The enemy spoke their loud words. We could claim Thorkil's body and do for him what befitted a king, but, on pain of being taken as slaves, we must be gone before nightfall. As I gave the order, Vasser shook his head, saying he had already sent warriors to attend to it. I asked Asa to go, but she was too late: Vasser had seen to everything. My father's body had been placed in his ship. As soon as Vasser's men pushed Thorkil's deathboat into the sea, Vasser said: 'Now we must leave. We must go now! The boats are ready. We shall go to Eng-land.'

'*Eng-land?*' At that time, I thought that Eng-land was another battlefield. We would simply leave one war for another.

'The north is already under Viking rule—Halfdan is king—' Vasser spluttered impatiently, 'and the south will soon follow. Guthrum will deal with Aelfred. Then the whole country will be ours. Come, get in the boat.'

'No.'

'Look, I know a safe place you can go to, not far inland, a good place, with water and wood, where you will not have to fight to settle. The Saxons there are quite willing to trade.'

He gestured to the crowd on the strand, some standing like stone, others restless, shuffling, gripping their sacks and waterskins. 'Your people are waiting. Tell them what to do. Give the order.'

Am I to rue giving the order to leave the Mark? Do I regret taking Vasser's advice? I should have made sure the barrels were full. Why didn't I think of the food?

Vasser spoke urgently, with his hands on my shoulders, his face too close to mine. His eyes were steel-grey like my father's, but where Thorkil's eyes held a welcome, a loving look of kindly attention, Vasser's eyes were cold.

'I will not have to fight in this Eng-land?' I said. 'What about you? Are you saying you're leaving us? Where will you go? We need your warriors.'

'I'll see you safely to land, then ride south to join Guthrum. I shall be back as soon as I can, with weapons and provisions, and I shall help you to trade with the Saxons. Look for me before Winternight.' Vasser touched my chin. 'Beren. Queen. Make sure you prepare a warm welcome—'

He spoke as if to extract some sort of promise and my blood ran cold. I pushed him back. 'Vasser Wulf. Father-brother. Don't give me orders.'

At this Vasser smiled. 'Get in the boat,' he said.

I shoved him away. 'We shall leave,' I said, 'after my father's deathrite is finished!' Vasser shrugged and stood back. 'We must burn Thorkil's body!'

I set fire to a dart. I raised my bow and fired it on to the boat, already adrift on the tide. 'Through fire to Valhal!' I shouted. Others took up the cry. 'Through fire to Valhal! Through fire to Valhal!' and Vasser was obliged to join in, nocking firedarts like the rest of us. Though few, we did our best: we filled the sky with them. Finally, when my father's deathboat was a small flame on the horizon, we gathered our belongings and boarded the ships. We crossed the sea.

Vasser was right. In the two months following our landing, we did not have to fight Saxons; we face a different enemy.

The time comes to prepare for Winternight, that time between leaf fall and winter cold, when we give thanks for good harvest, full barns and barrels. We should mark it with several days' feasting, but our boards will remain bare, unless I find food. Asa's barrels are empty.

For the first time I heard fear in her voice when she laid out for me what was left—a few rotting apples, some few bowlfuls of grain, spoilt by seawater during the voyage, meat so high it moved by itself. There were tears in her eyes—she told me she had caught a chill— but she smiled too much and looked away as she spoke. She could not hide the truth: she, who tried to be both mother and father to me, was afraid.

So am I. It is not something a queen should admit, but it is true. I am afraid. If we do not find fresh food, we shall all starve.

We shall not die. I shall feed my people. I, Berengeria, daughter of Thorkil, so swear. As I spoke these brave words to myself, I took a draught of river water from my water pouch, to ease the ache away from my belly.

My thoughts turned again to my uncle, Vasser Wulf. When he came, he would challenge me for the crown, I knew it, so I sent up a quick prayer: 'Great Othinn, hear me. Keep Vasser Wulf in the south, at least until I have eaten a respectable meal. My sword arm is weak!'

Like a monster from the slime of a stagnant pond, a much darker thought rose from the deep of my mind. Vasser would take the crown by a path other than combat: he would take me as his queen.

The monster spread its vile poison in mind pictures: Vasser at the feast with me at his side, Vasser demanding that I, as his wife, pass round the ale-horn. Vasser bedding me.

He would marry me. He wanted to rule me. He wanted me to bow down to him.

'*Never!*' The word escaped my lips and a flock of starlings shot up from the tops of the trees. Shocked, I glanced round, watched and waited, until quiet fell again over the wood. Like a soulspirit, an owl hooted. Winter comes.

I scrambled to my feet, fearworms fretting my mind. My hawk, Raed, had been gone too long. Had she been felled by a Saxon dart? Or had she chosen to go her own way? Like all hunters, I feared that one day my hawk would fly free from my wrist and never come back.

Tss. Tss. Tsss, I called, using our own special signal, but Raed did not answer, nor come gliding to my hand. Daylight was fading fast. *Tss. Tss.* Was she confused by the twilight? Had I left it too late? Skar the fowler should also have returned to the wood by now.

Skar, my hunting companion and my friend. When we crossed the sea, it was Skar who insisted on bringing all the hawks and their cages; they had to be caged separately for fear of their tearing each other as we tossed over the waves. Some objected to the hawks taking up so much room, as against the dogs, the sheep and goats, that we had to leave behind, but I took his part, knowing that the hawks were needful for hunting, and Skar, an old man of some forty years, was thankful for that. Skar is a silent man—Vasser had his tongue slit for what he took as an insolent comment— but I would have Skar at my side in any battle. Vasser took his tongue, but not his strong right arm and his fiery spirit, and his skill with the hawks. With his hawk, Blackwing, Skar had followed the track north by the river, to a little pool where I had seen a hare come to drink.

I pressed on through the trees and sent up more prayers. 'Great Othinn, hear me. Keep Skar safe! Othinn, shield him from harm. Great Othinn, protect our hawks, Raed and Blackwing!'

CHAPTER 2
CAPTURE

The river, a safe crossing back to our camp, lay behind me, two or three hundred paces. Ahead, too near for comfort, on the other side of the wood, was the Saxon village. I say village, though the houses were mere hovels, fit only for beggars, with rotting thatch and tumbledown walls. There were old clearings in the woods, trees chopped and mossy piles of old kindling, signs of a once-thriving community, but there were few inhabitants. I saw women, children, old and sick only. Perhaps the men had gone south, to war.

Cedd was leader of these inhabitants, tall, thickset, with a permanent frown, but not yet full-bearded. In the first few days after we arrived, I had spied on Cedd. I saw him help an old woman gather leaves for fresh bedding and draw water from the well. I saw him drilling a small band of young ones, maidens and youths, who, though skilled with bow and dart, still had much to learn about fighting. Cedd did his best to teach them. He was patient and a good leader of those left in his charge, some of whom showed their hatred for Vikings. One of the drills was to run with drawn sword at a straw figure of a man. One lad, the strongest of all, with the thighs of a bull, dressed the figure up in Viking helm and shield, then stabbed at the figure with a short sword, over and over again, until it was unrecognizable.

I tilted my head to scan the darkening sky. Had Raed left the wood? I could be searching for her for hours at night in strange territory, and Asa would say: *'Queens should not put themselves at risk for their hawks'*; and I should reply, *'Dearly loved stepmother, that may be true of other queens, but not Berengeria.'* I was not going back without my hawk.

Then, like a sign from the gods, Raed was there, an unmistakable black cross in the sky. She took stand over a clearing and stared down at her prey. As always, I held my breath to watch her plunge to it, straight and unerring, like a speeding dart, then I ran to where she waited, one yellow claw raised and firmly hooked into the back of a fine plump hare. As usual it was a clean kill, one swift snap of her beak into the soft spot between the bones of the hare's neck. It didn't suffer.

Rewarding her with a scrap of meat from my pouch, I lifted the prey, wrapped it in cloth and tied it over my shoulder. I stroked Raed's feathers, took her on to my wrist and spoke soft words in her ear. *'One more. One more.'* Then I threw her up again. *'With Othinn!'* I called after her, and within a breath, she was gone.

Night gathered in the trees. It was dangerous to stay much longer. I turned full circle, scanning for Raed, then when I called her, Skar answered, sending a warning with his low croak. *Kraak. Kraak. An enemy. Close by.*

Skar's pale face emerged between trees, fifty paces away. *Raed?* I signalled urgently and he poked his fingers at the sky, to say he had sight of both hawks, Raed and Blackwing, and would take them safely back to the river. I ran to him.

'If I'm not back by dawn, cross the river—you, and Helga and Asa—come on horseback but carry no weapons—' Skar raised his eyebrows, so I repeated my instruction—*'no weapons.'* Skar gave a quick nod. 'Ask for me at the Saxon village. If I'm killed, take Brand as leader. Go!' On his way, Skar shot a glance over his shoulder, then jerked his arm—*They're coming! Run! Run!*

I didn't run. To give Skar time to get away, I stood my ground as weaving shadows became a dozen youths crashing towards me. An iron torc on the leader's throat glinted in the last rays of the sun. It was Cedd. He had a sword in his hand. I could have drawn mine too and ended it there and then. Instead, it was then that I turned and ran for the river.

I threw down the hare, hoping they would stop to take it for themselves, and so gain me a few precious minutes, but they didn't falter. Wherever I ran, they were there, cutting off my escape.

Like hounds on a fox, they forced me down the path they had chosen. When, through the dark cage of trees, I glimpsed the moon, a whole round full moon, my heartjump told me where I was headed.

I'd lingered long enough, hidden in the bushes on the edge of their firepit to know that Cedd's favourite stories were about the full moon and the Hill. The Hill is a steep grassy mound, a landmark on the coast north of the river, a massive knoll, three times the height of a mast, four times the width of a trading ship. Its western slope that comes down to the edge of the Saxon wood, divided from it by a well-worn track, is unbroken, with no outcrops, but, set in the middle, almost at the top, is a single black hole, a dark mouth of an entrance, that gapes wide as a whale's jaw.

Cedd said there were demons inside the Hill. Under a full moon, he said, they came hunting, black-tongued dragons, hungry for human flesh, servants of an old and dark magic. He told such tales. Had he known I was listening? Had he wanted to scare me? Did he think I was scared now? Yes, I was scared, but I made fear my friend, to put fire into my spirit, and I thumped my feet into the ground. *Old Magic. Dead magic.* I wasn't scared of any demons. Never. My head was clear about that, but my blood said otherwise and it chilled and spiked, as if it had turned to frost in my veins.

Cedd thudded after me. No word was spoken. Then—*Thump Thump Thump*—Cedd beat a stone on his leather shield. I knew what it meant. He was signalling the end of the hunt, as if I were already his prisoner. The signal was for all of us, hunters and prey, to stand to and suffer the outcome.

I replied to his challenge by shouting out the names of the trees as I passed. *Ash, elm, birch, oak! Askr . . . almr . . . birk . . . eik!* I shouted the names like a shield spell, to protect me before battle—Danish words to shut out his Saxon racket—but I was still forced to run in the direction

Cedd had chosen for me, and, when the trees thinned, I found myself crossing the track to the foot of the Hill. As Cedd and his gang came out of the wood, I turned to face them.

The moon, standing high over us, was a frigid arbiter. In its clear light, Cedd and his followers, all untried youths aged between ten and fifteen summers, all, save Cedd, weaponless, proudly brandishing their sharp sticks and stones, lined up at the edge of the trees. On the other side of the track, I crossed my hands in front of me and touched knife and axe, both tucked into my belt. If any of them rushed forward I would deal with him, but no one moved. Then Cedd pointed over my shoulder at the Hill and gestured that I should turn and face it.

Across the hearth fire, Cedd Grimface had leaned to his listeners, as if to share a deep secret. *'Once there was a traveller,'* he said, *'who strayed on to the Hill after dark. He was after the round white moon. He thought he would be able to grab it and bring it down to the ground, like a fat bladder.'* Cedd drew his fingers up into claws and bent over the flames. *'The demons got him,'* he said, *'(Snatch.) They put worms in his head and snakes in his belly. (Groan. Writhe.) Which ate up his insides. (Teeth grinding and cheeks sucking.) Leaving the juicy flesh for a demon-dinner. There was no trace of him, afterwards, not a bone, not a fingernail.'* He paused for the pictures to form in our heads, then went on, *'Full Moonrise is Demonrise. When the demons come looking for their supper. They can suck the life out of you by touching you with one finger, on any part of your bare skin.'*

Now I glanced at the slope and its dark opening. *'Demons,'* Cedd murmured. *'How brave are you, Viking?'*

I swung round to answer him. 'Brave enough!' I called, using their Saxon tongue. At this, the line of youths stirred like rushes in the wind.

'Go on then!' he said, indicating the Hill.

I glowered back at the slope. Tales, tall tales, to make you shiver on a winter's night, at home, round the fire. *Demonrise.* The demons would have to catch me first and I can run like the wind.

'Go on, Danish!' Cedd shouted. 'Climb the Hill!'

I faced Cedd again, then took my time to lock stares with each of his men, saving my hardest, longest stare for Cedd himself.

For answer, he rapped on his shield and the others took up the beat, slapping their free hands on the front of their thighs, shouting: *'On! On! On! On!'*

No fight then, but a challenge. Lifting my hands from my weapons, I raised my fists to Othinn, to claim his protection, then turned back to the Hill. Now it was a mass of darkness, like a louring black wave of the sea about to fall and wash me away. I put my hand on my hammering heart and began to climb.

CHAPTER 3
THE HILL

The Hill was longer than I thought, and steeper, and my legs soon burned with the effort. Like a fish out of water, I gasped for breath, the opening as far away as when I began, but I knew Cedd would be watching for any sign of weakness, so I kept climbing.

A stitch pain bent me double so that I didn't see the stone pillar until I hit it. My right hand cracked, as it met the stone, and I bit my lip at the pain. There was a loud sigh from the gang. Like a warning, the tall finger of granite blocked my path. This must be the place Cedd had spoken of in his stories, the stone to which people were tied, before being killed as offerings to the demons, in old time, long gone. I screwed up my eyes to examine the stone, feeling for marks. There were no marks: no grooves from a blade, no scratches. In moonlight, it shone clean, and struck me as solid and certain.

The watchers were silent. What did Cedd expect to happen? That I would fall dead at the foot of the stone? That it would somehow grow arms and strike me down?

The bloodstone—that was Cedd's name for it—towered over me like a giant's finger. I had seen the same in the Mark, set there by the people from old time. To what purpose? No one knew. Perhaps they kept ward. *This far and no further. Stop now. Don't go on.* I placed my hot hands on the stone.

Thump. Thump. Cedd beat on his shield. *On! On! On!* He and his gang stood in a line at the foot of the slope, ready to climb after me. I slapped the stone hard with both hands, then shook my fists at my pursuers. *Go no further. Here be Demons.* Old Magic. Dead Magic. *Thump. Thump.*

Demons. I didn't believe in them, but Cedd did. As he came up the slope, I threw back my head and my arms and hands wide. 'OTHI . . . I . . . I . . . NN!' I howled up at the stars. 'OTHI . . . I . . . INN!' I howled like a wolf. 'OTHI . . . I . . . INN!'

With a quick gesture, I drew the knife from my belt and flourished it above my head as if to cut out a piece of the darkness. 'GRE . . . EAT OTH . . . I . . . I . . . NN! BRING OUT THE DEMONS!' I yelled.

Thuuuuuuump. Cedd made a rattling sound on the drum, and behind me something moved. I flicked my head round, scanning over my shoulder. There was a slight noise, a rustle of leaves, a scuff of the ground. An animal perhaps, an owl or a badger? The smooth silver hump of the Hill loomed above me, the demons' door at its heart.

Torches flared at the foot of the slope, as the gang members passed fire to each other. I let the flames take all my attention, which was a mistake.

'Great Odin's not listening,' shouted Cedd. 'The demons won't come at your command, you should have gone into the cave.' His wide blunt face grimaced with scorn, as, from the shoulders of the Hill, on either side, his followers sprang out. They had outflanked me. Even as I uselessly threw my knife, even as I was caught and dragged back to the bloodstone, I couldn't help admiring the strategy.

'Begga begga begga begga—' they chanted like madmen, as they wound cords round my wrists, then tied me to the stone. 'Magga magga magga magga—' It took four to hold me, while the others danced, waving their torches. As they drew the cords tight, I kicked, I shouted. I ducked and hit out with heels and head, but a blow to the temple knocked the sense from me, and they soon had me fastbound, and the leather tunic stripped from my back. I could do nothing but endure, so I hugged the stone and froze my mind, stone-cold, for the beating.

I still had my voice. 'Rot in a stinking pit!' I shouted as their bramble whips touched my back. The words, spoken in their own Saxon tongue, caused some to pause. 'Drown in poison!' I spat.

'Be quiet, Viking!' Cedd's voice was quiet, but iron-hard.

'Hope it burns your guts out—' I yelled, then, '*Ugh!*' I bit my tongue at the sudden sting of the first stroke. Steadying myself for the next, head high, I took the beating. Three strokes and I knew it was nothing worse than I'd had from my uncle Vasser, for letting the hearthfire go out, or for burning his dinner.

'*Begga begga begga*—' All the while I was being tormented, the gang kept up their mindless chant. 'Magga

magga magga—' Was this a cry to some god? Or a battle yell to rouse the blood? I focused on it and was able to predict when each blow would fall, as the beater kept up the rhythm. Five strokes, six. My shirt ripped. There was a trickle of blood. They would pay for my blood.

'Begga begga—'

The chanting stopped as if chopped by an axe. No one moved. Then there was a low gasp and a stifled cry. I strained my neck to see and grazed my face on the stone, but all I saw was the black shoulder of the Hill and above it a few stars. Then someone screamed out the word:

'DEMON!' The gang fled down the slope, shouting, 'Demon . . . demon . . . DEMON!'

Behind me a great roar sounded out, a monster's roar, hollow and echoing like a hunting horn, but louder and deeper than any horn I'd ever heard. I strained at my bonds. *Demon?* I didn't believe in such things. It was a trick, to frighten me. I waited for the next step. Would the demon appear, with fangs dripping blood to sink into my flesh, or would it be a wraith, with talons like ice-cold needles, stretched ready to pluck out my gizzard? I smiled. I hadn't thought Cedd so inventive.

Then someone cut my bonds and I fell back from the stone. My body shook, but it wasn't fear. It was the trembling that comes after wrestling or hard running, it soon settles, but it stopped me from moving quickly. For several breaths, I was weak, and that led to my downfall.

When I managed to stand up and step away from the stone, I stumbled and ended back on my knees. A heavy wool cloak, stinking of sheep fat, was thrown over me. With a roar, I was punching my way free, then I fell again, tangled in the folds of the cloak.

A cold hand helped me upright and arranged the cloak over my shoulders, so that I could look out from under the rim of its broad black hood. The newcomer passed me my knife.

'Who are *you*?' I said.

'I'll explain everything later,' said the stranger, in my own tongue, in my own Danish tongue. I looked at him in surprise but saw only a black-cloaked figure as he stepped forward and raised both arms like black wings.

'Go home!' he called down to Cedd and his men. 'Come not nigh the demons! I must deal with them alone!' He lifted a huge horn to his mouth and blew into it. It made the sound of a thousand horses at the gallop. It was thunder: it was the fart of Thor.

Cedd made no move. Again the horn sounded.

'I hold the demons at bay with this noise,' shouted the stranger. 'They hate this noise! I don't know how much longer I can keep them from coming out. They must be *ravenous* by now.'

At this Cedd's men fell back, but Cedd laughed and held his position, so the stranger repeated his warning. 'I can hear them, Cedd. Their bellies rumble like thunder. Go home while you can.'

'What about the Viking?' Cedd shouted. 'She was stealing our food, trespassing—'

'I have her in charge. I shall speak to Father Anselm about this. You need trouble yourself no more, Cedd. Go home now.'

As the stranger lifted the horn again, ready to blow, he whispered, 'You need fear no demons. Wait inside the cave.' I stood my ground. 'Go on!' he said. 'There's food in there. Go!' As the terrible blast sounded again, I snatched up my tunic and made my way up the slope.

If there weren't any demons, why had the stranger said there were? It seemed a cruel trick.

The cave was wide and empty, no more than seven or eight strides across. In spite of the stranger's assurance, fearworms roiled in my belly, so I walked them away, pacing to and fro near the entrance, crossing the moon-beams that shone there, and listened as every footfall, every breath, echoed back to me. This place had its own way with sounds.

The stranger came back. He lit several torches, push-ing the oil-soaked bundles of reeds into cracks in the wall, then stood looking down on to the Hill.

'Who are you?' I said, but he held up his hand.

'I want to be sure they're not still lurking around. It's for their own good, but I know Cedd, he takes no notice of homecall.'

'Homecall?'

'Yes, that's why I'm here. On patrol along the sea path and—luckily for you—the Hill is one of my posts, for sounding the homecall.'

'I've heard it and wondered who made the call.'

'We sound the horn to—'

'—tell everyone to get safe under cover for the night,' I said.

'Yes, and to let Father Anselm back at the monastery know all is well. Ah, listen.' He gestured me to his side. There was the repeated call of a hunting horn in the distance. 'That's Lucius sounding homecall from Top Acre. There it goes again. We're supposed to sound the horn three times in all. There, that's the third. All is well. Don't you have the same thing in the Mark?'

'Our horns are nothing like that—' I pointed to the great horn at his side.

'Impressive, huh? This is a shell trumpet. They're used a lot by Greek hill farmers, I believe, and the peoples of the Far Eastern plains—Huns, Goths, men of Dacia—I made this one myself. You have to make a hole to blow into, in the side of the shell. I used an auger—Look.' With both hands, he held out the great shell for me to see, then, before I had time to examine it properly, he set it down. 'Forgive me.' His voice faded and his face reddened. 'I think everyone's as interested in these things as I am. It's a grievous fault.' He sighed. 'I shall be in trouble, for using the shell for homecall, and not my horn—' he tapped the smaller horn hanging from his belt, '—when I get back to the monastery.'

'Why did you use it then? To scare Cedd? I don't think it worked.'

'It seems to have impressed the others—'

'—along with the demon story—'

'Look, I have my reasons for keeping them away from the Hill. It isn't a safe place for them at the moment.'

The stranger smiled and held out his right hand in greeting. 'I forget myself. Welcome. I am Albinus, monk apprentice of the monastery of St Bede's, under the tutelage of my master, Father Anselm.'

I gripped his forearm.

'Berengeria, daughter of Thorkil,' I said. *'Vestu hal.'*

CHAPTER 4

THE CRACKS OF NIFLHEIM

'**T**hrough there. Go on. No demons remember, I promise!' Albinus laughed as I hesitated to move to the back of the cave. Where the shadows struck deepest, there were two large gaping cracks, splitting the wall from top to bottom. Albinus pointed to the one on the left. 'Through there. It's not far. I'll douse the rest of the torches,' he said.

I thought I could trust the monk apprentice, he seemed friendly enough and someone I could talk to, who would listen to me and perhaps act as a go-between in our dealings with the Saxons. Christians had visited my father Thorkil's court in the Mark; they were peace-loving people. But was it wise to go with a stranger, inside the Hill? Was it a trap? I had never been in such a place. Would I end up in Hel itself? In deepest Niflheim, in the realm of worst cold and darkness?

I had just gathered enough courage to poke my torch inside the crack, when Albinus joined me. 'I've a few minutes before I have to sound homecall from the next post, by the river. Let's eat.' Stepping ahead into the opening, he said, smiling, 'Will you join me for supper, Berengeria?'

'Thank you, Albinus,' I replied, and when he had turned and walked into the dark tunnel, I cast a quick prayer to great Othinn and followed.

The path was lit only by our two wavering torches. To keep my spirit from weakness, I counted my steps—fifty-two—until the tunnel opened out into a wide space. The path did not take me to Hel's gate then, but into an inner cave, much bigger than the first.

'You soon get used to the dark, but you must always take care. There are so many caves here, it's easy to lose yourself.' I laughed as the fear shook my belly. 'Light more torches, if it would make you feel better.'

Albinus had made this inner cave into a homely sanctuary, with sacks of food supplies, a stack of kindling, and fresh water. 'Sit,' he said, like a host inviting a guest to the hearth, laying sticks and dried grass for a fire. He was at ease here, but I was not. I was shivering.

The cave cut off the sounds that I heard every night without knowing, until they were absent: the last bird calls, the fluster of wings as the rooks went home to their nests, the windbreath in the trees, the shift of badger and fox. To find courage I talked.

'I've seen you before,' I said. 'When we first landed. You watched us land.'

'Not me,' said Albinus, without looking up from his food sack. He passed me some bread and cheese and I'm ashamed to say that I sank my teeth into it like a bear. 'Not me,' he repeated.

It was you, I thought stubbornly, as I tore at the bread. *As we came in to land, I stood on the prow of the boat, keeping*

watch on the figure on the cliff top, as he appeared and disap-
peared with each rise and fall of the tide. The man, as I took it to
be, stood ward perhaps, a sentry on the eastern defences. He was
not arrayed as a warrior, though, but was only an anonymous
dark presence in a long black cloak, the hood pulled low over his
face. Once we had beached the boats and set off on the trek
inland, he came with us; I knew it, though all I saw—twice—
was a shape, a movement against the lie of the wind, sliding
between the trees as we came through the wood. He kept his
distance. No one else saw and I didn't draw their attention to
him. If need be I would deal with any threat. We had enough to
concern us.

All the way from the strand to the place where we set down
our burdens, we were watched by the stranger who came and
went like a wraith.

I studied Albinus as he lit more torches, wedging
them securely into the rocky walls. The monk's habit
he wore fell in deep folds round his ankles and he
tugged it up round his waist, and tied a tighter knot in
the cord, securing it and showing his bare feet. An iron
cross hung on his chest. His face was thin and pale,
with dark shadows under his eyes. His cropped head
was covered with a lint of fair hair, startlingly fair,
almost white.

'A secret den, huh?' I said, between mouthfuls.
'Food, water, torches—all the supplies you need, a
good hiding-place. Is that why you keep Cedd away, so
you can keep it for yourself?'

'No, it isn't.' Albinus gave me a stern look. 'I keep
Cedd at bay for his own good. I'm a student of medicine

and alchemy—for the past month or so I've been working on a particularly dangerous firepowder, a recipe I translated from the Greek—well, I won't bore you with the details—but the ingredients could be harmful if they fell into the wrong hands. It's for the best that Cedd is prevented from coming here.'

'So you invented the tale of the demons?'

'I didn't have to. Cedd invented it. He and his friends witnessed the result of one of my experiments—a great explosion of fire and smoke from the Hill. Cedd invented the "demons" to explain what they'd seen. That was clever of him. As leader, he was expected to explain it and show no fear, and he has a gift for telling stories so real that they are taken for gospel truth. He was afforded free meals, too, while he spread the tale round the village. After that everyone gave the Hill a wide berth, until tonight.'

Until I, a hated Viking, trespassed into his territory to steal his food, I thought, but said nothing. Instead I muttered my thanks for cutting me free from the bloodstone, but Albinus seemed not to hear. He merely chuckled and the cave walls echoed the sound.

'It was an impressive explosion—better than demons. I foolishly left a flask containing a small amount of fire-powder in the middle of the embers, here.' Albinus sat down on the opposite side of the fire and stared into the flames. 'I was almost to the monastery when I heard the blast! It very near blew the top of the Hill away! Now I tease Cedd by going along with his tale, blowing the shell trumpet and pretending to fight the demons, and he's no longer sure whether they exist or not. I'll tell him the truth when I'm ready. I just need a little more time. Then it's *demon doom*!'

We sat and ate together in silence, deep in our own separate thoughts.

One thought rose above the rest in my mind. 'How do you come to speak Viking?' I said. 'You are not from the Mark.' Albinus had the brown skin and straight nose of someone from the south, from one of those sun-kissed lands Thorkil had told me about.

'It's what I'm good at,' he replied. 'I seem to be able to pick up languages at one go—Greek, Latin, Saxon, Viking, even Celtish, though not so much of that is spoken here. How come you to speak Saxon?'

'Back in the Mark, I had a Saxon nurse. She taught me her language alongside my own. Truthfully, the two tongues are not so different.' Albinus passed me more cheese.

'You had a nurse? Royal family were you?'

'Agh!' I jumped up, pretending to have burnt myself, as I reached over the fire for the cheese. I was not sure that I was ready to reveal my true identity or share all my history.

'Hold out your arm!' Albinus doused my arm with cold water, twisting it this way and that to find my 'burn'. He dabbed a couple of likely spots with a wet cloth, then gave up. 'A simple "I don't want to talk about it" would have done, you know,' he said.

I flushed and shook my head, alarmed that he had seen through my foolish attempt at deception.

'Your name—is it truly Albinus?'

'That's what the Father Abbot called me—for obvious reasons—' he patted the pale lint on his head, 'when I was brought to the monastery as a baby, but I'm usually called Albi, unless I'm in trouble with the tutor monks. Then it's *ALBINUS*!' I laughed as he mimicked the thunderous voice of one of his teachers.

'What about Berengeria?' he said, reaching over to poke flames from the embers. 'That's a name from southern Iberia, not from cold northern lands.' Startled, I recalled something my father Thorkil had said to me: *Make a friend of the one who knows your name.* When I had questioned him further, he said that it would be evidence of someone with a broad and learned mind, with the curiosity of a traveller, of someone with stories to share.

I stared at Albinus, as he watched the fire, intent on his food.

'You're right,' I said, lightly. 'My name is from the south. From a land where the sun shines, *"on green vineyards and a warm blue sea"*. My father named me.'

'Berengeria.'

My face grew hot. Albinus pronounced my name as if it were precious, just as my father had. *Thorkil*. He was not long dead and I missed him. There had not yet been time to grieve for him.

I took a long draught of cold water. 'Beren,' I said. 'Just call me Beren.'

Albinus picked up a torch and went back to the opening into the tunnel. 'I have to finish my patrol.

I won't be long; then, before you go back across the river, I'll treat those cuts on your back.'

As he left the inner cave, I took up a torch and followed. 'I'll keep watch,' I said. I would not sit alone in the dark, demons or no.

'As you will,' said Albinus, setting off down the Hill at a brisk pace.

I won't be long; drink before we go back inside the
river. I'll hear them rub us, poor boy.'

As he felt the inner cave, broke up a rock, and tell-
ance. 'I'll keep watch,' said. 'I would not sit along in
the dark, dejected or on.

'As you will,' said Sámus, settling self down the hill.
a-hing off.

CHAPTER 5
THE FOX

How long I stood there, looking down on the moonlit Hill, I'm not sure. What made me turn to look back inside the cave? Was it a sound? Or a scent? Perhaps, being chilled, I thought to go back to the fire again. Perhaps I thought of the food I had left there. Whatever the reason, I turned and saw the fox. A dog fox, by the size of him. Two eyes, gold lamps, stared straight at me from the back of the cave. There was no mistaking the smell—that fox stink. He watched me and I made no move; then, when I saw him step into the tunnel, I knew I must follow.

I thought it was the same tunnel, leading to Albinus's sanctuary, but it was not. It was the wrong crack, the wrong tunnel. This wormhole of darkness went on and on, much further than the other, and the cold, hard rock closed all around me, and held me like a mouth that was swallowing me whole. *Too close, too close.* Bent low, my head and haunches were on a level; I shuffled forward, my knees burning with the effort. There was no sign of the fox and I should have gone back when I could, then I couldn't turn myself round and there was nothing to do but go forward.

Water glistened on the smooth grey walls. It was

ice-cold and silent. A fearworm whispered that I might never get out, that I had been led here by a demon, a shapeshifter, taking an animal form, that I would be trapped here for ever.

I must mark the path. I shone the torch on the ground at my feet, then reached for my knife. It was too firmly wedged in my belt, so I scraped at the floor with my fingers and uncovered a gleam of white pebbles. When I'd picked out a handful, I pressed on, and let them fall, one by one by one. The tunnel swerved, left and right, but so slowly that it was hard to remember every change. By luck or by fate, I had no need of my pebbles: there were no side tunnels, or forks in the path; it led only one way. When I finally emerged into a space where I could stand up, I held my torch high and examined the new cave.

Albinus's sanctuary was large, but this was much bigger, hollow and empty, like the inside of a skull that has been scoured clean by the weather. There was only one exit, so I was not lost, though the fearworm in my gut continued to writhe and throw its sour bile to the back of my throat.

Water ran, in thin chalky trickles, down the walls of the cave. As I stood still to listen, to my great joy, I heard the sea itself. The tide pounded the base of the Hill on its eastern side, like a great heartbeat, the sound I grew up with and heard every day of my life in the Mark.

With a soft rush a memory washed over me, as I heard again the west wind sweeping over the Mark at spring tide. Asa and I on the shore, shielding our eyes to scan the horizon, as we waited for my father's ship to ride back to us.

Thorkil. My king-father. His body lying in state on his ship and my giving the signal to let loose the fire darts, in so dense a storm that the smoke from his pyre hid the sun.

Thorkil. The memory disarmed me. I closed my eyes, bowed my head. Thorkil was gone, his body given to the sea. Asa and I were here now: we had left the Mark and would never go back.

My torch flared and sank low, and before I could save it, the fire was gone.

The darkness was complete. I had not anticipated this pitch black, where there were no visible markers to guide me. When the torch went out, I had been facing the tunnel. I hadn't moved, merely turned my head, this way and that, so I should still be facing the same way. If I put out my hands I would surely be able to find it. Slowly, I shuffled forward, my arms outstretched and, within a couple of breaths, felt the rock and pressed myself to it. Then I felt for the opening.

Unbroken, the wall went on. Step after step, I felt my way along it, expecting my fingers to fall, with the next breath, into the empty space of the tunnel. All I felt was the rock. Then I crawled on my hands and knees, using my fingers like a webspinner's arched legs, testing each inch of dirt on the floor to find the tunnel.

The fox walked into the cave. *Pad-pad-pad.* I slid myself up the wall. 'Halloo!' I called loudly, hoping the noise would scare him. My voice thundered and echoed back to me. 'Halloo . . . loo . . . alloo.'

The fox snuffled and pad-padded across the cave again. That stink, rank and warm. *Fox*. I drew my knife. I had never known a fox attack, but I was taking no chances. *Pad-pad-pad*—then silence. It was close, no more than a stride away: I could hear it breathe—but it had stopped moving and, for a while, we stayed put, both of us, guests of the dark.

'Halloo! Halloo! Where are you?' The fire of a torch flickered towards me down the tunnel. Albinus, returning from homecall patrol, as he had said he would. As his light pierced the darkness, I looked for my fox. There was no sign of him.

'What are you doing here in the dark?' Albi eyed the knife in my hand. The remains of my torch lay at his feet. He took a new one from his belt, lit it and passed it to me. 'I *thought* you might lose your way. It's easy in this place.'

'I was quite safe,' I said, sharply. I tucked my blade back in its sheath. 'Did you see the fox?'

'*Fox?* Why would a fox come in here? Especially with you poking around.'

'There was a fox! A dog must have chased it in, or a wolf.'

'Or a boar! Or a stag! Or a Welsh dragon! Perhaps there really are demons who eat foxes for dinner!'

'Shut up!'

'You're not making any sense. Here, let me see,' Albi said in a professional tone. As he touched my forehead lightly with cold fingers, I tossed my head like an angry goat. 'Over-choleric, I should say.'

'I'm perfectly well!'

'Then what's this about foxes?'

'There was a fox,' I said. 'I shall prove it!' I held the torch out over the dusty cave floor. 'There must be tracks.'

'No tracks. Not a one.'

I examined the floor and found nothing.

'Can't you smell it?' I could no longer detect the stink myself.

'Are you sure you're well? You look pale.'

'It's the light,' I mumbled.

Albi shone his torch round the walls of the cave. 'You've seen something, haven't you? Was it a demon? I can help you there. Stand back.'

Albi lifted a large iron cross from his chest and solemnly went to stand in the middle of the cave. *'Abi, diabole horribilis! Nunc! Nunc!'* he shouted, sweeping the cross to and fro high in the air.

'Unc! Unc!' came the echo.

'What sort of gibberish is that?' I said. I stood up and pulled my belt tight.

'It's not gibberish—it's Latin. *Nunc! Nunc!*' Albi shouted.

'Unc! Unc!' was the reply.

I started to giggle. 'You'd better keep that cross still, unless—unless you want the demon to go *cross-eyed*!' A shout of laughter burst from me and shook me like a dog with a rag. I bent over, holding my knees. Albi stared at me, then he too laughed out loud.

'That would be a start,' he said. He put his arm round my shoulders and led me to the exit, then, still chortling, pushed me in front of him down the tunnel.

Together we stood outside the cave entrance and looked down the slope of the Hill. The night was still and clear, the sky filled with bright stars.

'I should treat those cuts for you—' said Albinus.

I shook my head. 'You've done enough. Tell me about Cedd,' I said. 'Why does he hate Vikings?'

I asked the question though I guessed the answer. Cedd's hatred was deep and particular. Dreading his words, yet needing to hear them, I waited for Albi to speak.

'Cedd lost his family in a Viking raid. They were all killed. Mother, father, and two older brothers.' We sat down and I prepared to hear the whole story.

'His father was headman of the village. There was no need for the raid, the Saxons here have not resisted the Vikings. They are practical people and look to the future. The north already lies under Viking rule and though Aelfred may yet win the south, he does not have the manpower to conquer all England. The folk here know that they will fare better to live in peace and feed their families, even if they sit under Viking rule. Halfdan of Jorvik is a fair king, he has not troubled us. I take it you will not trouble us?'

'No. We want peace as much as anyone. I've had enough of war.'

'Last spring, the raiders came out of nowhere. They attacked the monastery first, then the village. They fired all the fields, some only just showing the first shoots of a fine crop. Cedd's parents died defending their land. He has reason to hate Vikings.'

'I am sorry for it. I regret the raid and that my own people did such a thing. We are not all the same. There are good and bad in every tribe.' Albi nodded. 'Cedd—' I went on. 'He's alone now?'

'Yes. He won't leave the village. He could have found a home at St Bede's, at the monastery. He could have become a monk apprentice like me. It's not an easy life, mind, with plenty of hard work and prayers nine times a day—but at least there's a roof over your head and if the Vikings ever come back, there are stout gates—'

'*I am Viking*,' I said, colouring with shame and irritation. 'Are we all condemned the same?'

'I didn't mean—'

'Stop talking,' I said. 'You talk too much.'

'I do, don't I? It's all that silence, I expect. In the monastery.' I welcomed the change of topic.

'What are you supposed to do when it's the silence?' I said.

'Oh, think about the sick and pray for them. I'm not very good at it. I once kept it up for an inch of the candle, then found myself starting to mutter.'

'Shouldn't you be back there now? Won't you be punished?'

'If I'm caught.'

We sat keeping our own silence for a short time longer, then I got to my feet, and Albinus picked up his pack. He reached out to clasp my hand and wrist.

'Berengeria. Beren. I'm glad I met you,' he said, as if we were taking our leave from the meadhall. 'I'm sorry if I offended—' I shook my head to cut off his apology. 'I'm glad I told you about Cedd. At least now you know the way the wind blows for him and his band. I'll say a prayer for him and for all of us, and light a taper for peace.'

'Yes. Thank you.' I made to leave but Albinus stopped me, placing his hand on my shoulder.

'You have goods to trade?'

'Yes. Silver, cloth, knives—' *Whatever we could scrape together.*

'Bring your goods, tomorrow, to the trading-place— you know it? At the end of the village, on the northern road?' I nodded. 'Father Anselm will spread word. You should not have to steal your food. Or creep about in the dark.'

'We'll be there.'

A distant bell clanged like a fog warning.

'By our Lady, I'm late again.'

'What for?' I said, as we walked down the Hill.

'Just Vespers,' he said.

CHAPTER 6
AT THE TRADING PLACE

That night, I slept badly, hag-rid by a dream of a journey down a tunnel, of a fox, and a fight with a secret enemy, whose flesh turned to smoke, whenever my blow struck home.

Othinn protect me. The familiar words, spoken as soon as I woke, were a comfort. Of all the gods Othinn is my favourite. He is wise, having given one of his eyes to drink the water of wisdom from the spring of Mimir. He discovered writing sign by hanging for nine days from the tree Ygdrassil. Best of all are his ravens, Huginn and Muninn, Thought and Memory, bringing him all the news from around the whole world, so he keeps in touch with us and our doings. I prayed Huginn to carry my thoughts to him.

The dream left me tired. Carefully, I made the offering of honey ale, pouring it on to the embers, raising a hiss and a smoke that would take my request up to Othinn. *The fox . . . did it bring me a message? And the dream . . . Is an enemy near? Tell me.*

'Beren! Would you stow this basket for me, please?'
Asa's voice, like a cast line, hooked me back from the

edge of the trading place, where I was on the lookout for Cedd and his gang. In spite of Albinus's assurances, I would take no risks with our safety. Twelve of us came to the trade; I had chosen carefully who should come and who stay behind. I left Brand to guard the camp—though I was beginning to see, as Vasser had promised, that there was no Saxon force here to oppose us—and took for myself the part of safeguard at the trading place. I did not show my weapons, but kept knife and axe safely hidden under my cloak.

Like a mother goose, Asa fussed over the others, deciding who should stand where and who should sell what, and for what goods they should barter, at what cost. My stepmother, a king's wife, took to trading like a duck to a pond. If the gods were with her, we would go back with plenty of food. Smiling encouragement, I shoved her small basket of soapstone vessels under her stall.

The trading place was a patch of cleared land the length of two ships on all its sides. On the side opposite, where the Saxons stood, there were but six vendors, none I recognized from the village: an old woman selling ale, a one-legged man with bunches of dried herbs and berries, a woman of middle years, spinning wool at the side of a basket piled high with yarn, and another woman selling bread. An old man sat slightly apart from them with a stall of cheeses which he was wrapping in leaves, and a dog with a litter of puppies. Asa would not have let animals anywhere near the food, but the old man did not seem to care and the puppies were soon jumping up to sniff and paw at his wares. Near the stalls was a barrel, filled with water. A small girl stood next to it with a big ladle.

On our side of the square, we stood shoulder to shoulder, except Skar, who set up his stands of hawks at some distance from the rest. He had brought six to barter, and, as he took them one by one from their baskets and tied each to its perch, he was already pestered by children longing to touch their shiny feathers. Raed was with me, but, not wanting to scare off custom, I did not carry her on my shoulder or wrist. She sat on her perch by Asa's stall, and watched over the trading, keeping an eye on things I was powerless to see—mice nibbling wheat ears in the middle of a field, sparrows hopping on the thatch of a Saxon dwelling which to me was merely a brown shape in the distance.

Next to Asa's stall, where she placed her weighing scales and small store of silver, Helga and her kin laid out a few handfuls of rowan berries, freshly gathered, some crows' feathers, and some tied bundles of herbs for cooking and healing. Next to Helga, Finn and Geir sat carving dolls and whistles from hazel. Then there was Leif laying out lengths of rope, with little Gerd, who was more trouble than help, running off to look at the puppies, and having to be called sharply back each time. Sigrid displayed samples of cloth, then settled to spinning sheep's wool, dyed with bramble and onion skins. The purple and gold colours attracted some attention, but none offered to buy.

I stood with Asa, but kept close watch for Cedd. Today, he had not been at the river when we crossed at the ford, nor on the edge of the wood. With Albi's help I had escaped a serious beating, but the incident on the Hill could only have made things worse.

Asa's stall, with its tray of silver blades, brooches, and toothpicks, was set out under an awning that stretched from the front of a tent, made from cloth-covered branches. She was busy unwrapping everything she had to sell: bright clasps and brooches, daggers and hilts, tilting them against each other to show off the designs. The items for sale were all her own, gifts from my father, her royal brooches and arm-rings, torcs and buckles. She had re-forged broken pieces, and decorated them, well-skilled in carving the intricate swirling patterns, the long thin hounds swallowing their own tails, and the sign for Thor's hammer. I wasn't sure they would sell though. Like us, the Saxons here were in need of basic items for everyday living, not finery. She would be lucky to sell the soapstone, let alone anything as precious as silver. But everyone needs a bowl, don't they? So there was a chance.

Asa tested her scales with a couple of weights. Almost at once two women, Saxon travellers, approached the stall. Asa pulled some bracelets aside to push her scales forward. Arms still folded into their sleeves, the women looked over her goods. I caught a glance from one of them and her eyes dropped away, then she and her friend moved on. Asa shrugged at me and I gave her a wry smile. 'There are gulls fishing, but they're not ready to bite.' We shared a smile at her turn of phrase, spoken boldly like any court poet or skald.

As more travellers arrived, setting down pack and staff under a tree, Asa called out, in the Saxon tongue: 'Open for business! Fine silver here! Best rates. Test the quality of your silver! Best rates here!' The newcomers were too intent on relief after their journey to listen to sales talk, and moved away from the square to squat in the wood, before making straight for the water butt, then the stalls selling bread and cheese.

I watched customers ebb and flow across the market place like a tide. All passed us by. Finally a group of travellers on horseback swept into the square and stopped to sample the Saxon ale. One, dressed in finer clothes than the others, brought his horse over to Asa's stall and bent down to pick up one of the brooches. His face lit with interest. So it should, I thought. The brooch was one of Asa's finest, with an image of great Othinn's eight-legged horse, Sleipnir, carved into the silver: a piece made for a queen. After some discussion, the brooch was bartered for a bag of grain, and, when the man's servant handed over the goods, the deep lines on Asa's face lifted into a warm smile.

As the customer turned his horse away, Asa said to me: 'First catch of the day is the sweetest!' She gave me a questioning look. 'Time for you to draw the crowd?' she said.

'Oh, very well,' I said and moved to the front of the stall.

'Noble carls!' I shouted. One or two faces turned to look at me, pleased at the idea of being thought 'noble'. 'Gather round. Gather round.' As my audience assembled, I held up a bowl of green soapstone. 'Who would like this fine bowl?' I called. 'It's the prize in our contest. It's yours if you win.' By this time, folk were crowding so near that I was pushed against the stall, which wobbled, jostling the stock. 'Step back there!' I called. Asa steadied the stall and secured my bowls. 'Let the hound see the hare.' There was a ripple of laughter at this. 'Rest your bones,' I said and I gestured to them, like a skald to his audience, to sit where they could, on hay bales and stools, upturned baskets, or cross-legged on the ground.

'Get on with it then!' someone called.

'What's the contest?' called another. 'Is it wrestling? I'll wrestle you any time, Viking, bowl or no.'

I shrugged off this comment and held up my hand for peace. 'Not wrestling, no. Not your sort, anyway, but wrestling of a kind. I have a riddle for you. It's very hard.' My audience stared at me, their minds engaged by the word 'riddle' as I knew they would be. They had forgotten all about the bowl, but I went on with my prattle. 'Solve the riddle,' I said, 'and win the bowl.'

'Get on with it!' someone shouted and was shushed by the rest.

'I will,' I replied and called for their attention in the usual manner. *'Hwaet!'* I said. 'Listen, then!' They fell silent. *'What is it?'* I began, using the traditional words of riddling. *'What is it? Tell me.'* I paused for a breath, then gave them the riddle: *'The poor have it. The rich need it.'* I waited, then gave the last clue. *'If you eat it, you die.'*

For a while, they stayed silent, then someone shouted, 'Again!'

'Again?' I asked and several heads nodded. 'Once more, then. Once only.' A piglet squealed and a dog barked, but my audience kept their eyes on my face. 'Ready?' I said. Answering nods. *Hwaet!* Listen, then. *The poor have it. The rich need it . . . '* I paused, holding their stares. *'If you eat it, you die.'*

As the deep quiet of thought filled the marketplace, like the low humming of contented bees, suddenly I felt dizzy and seasick. Briefly I closed my eyes, then I heard something. A soft pad-padding across the hard ground. I opened my eyes.

In front of the crowd, the fox sat watching me. His mask, on his fine-boned face, was red from his ears to below his eyes and along his muzzle, then white on his chin and breast. His legs, fore and hind, were as thin as sticks. He bent, nosing for grubs in a clump of grass. Then, swift as a hawk, his head jerked up, his ears twisting to some sound that I couldn't hear, and his body dropped into a fighting crouch, his brush lying along the ground. He fixed his eyes on mine and raised his muzzle. There was no mistake. He had brought me a message. *Danger. A hidden threat. Trust no one. Stay alert.*

With long delicate steps he left and when he was gone, I heard voices shouting, as if from some distance. I shook my head.

'Poison!'

'Time!'

'Hard work!'

'*Wake up and tell us!*' The riddle! People in the market-place were shouting out their answers and grumbling that I must be brain-addled to sit as if stunned.

'Guess again!' I called, trying to remember which riddle I had given. After half-hearted attempts, they hissed at me and made rude gestures, then they drifted away. I glanced at Asa. 'Did you see the fox?' I said. 'It was so strange.'

Asa was speaking to a customer. When she had finished trading she shook her head. 'What fox?'

I scanned the marketplace, but there was no sign of it. A small hand tugged at my breeches.

'Are you a Viking?' the child asked.

'Yes,' I said, squatting down to look at him.

'What's the answer?'

'What answer?' I said. Startled by the look of disap-pointment in the child's face, I said, 'I'm sorry. It's nothing.'

'What?'

'It's nothing. The answer's *nothing*.'

Light dawned in his eyes and he grinned with pleas-ure. Then, even though he had not guessed the answer, I gave him the bowl.

As the day wore on, I thought about the fox. Was I sickening for some illness? Perhaps I was just hungry.

Eeek! Eeeek! Haaah! The nearby crowd broke apart as a piglet smeared with mud dashed through and dived under my stall.

'HOY!' I shouted, grabbing an empty basket. When it set off running again, I ran after it.

'Close the gap!' I said, gesturing to the crowd to close in on the pig which was now rooting under the bread stall. Pushing my open basket in front of me like a shield, I bent down to capture it. The piglet squealed and squawked, but I followed its every twist and turn. As if knowing the chase was over, it let loose its water in protest, but I held on and pushed the basket closer until it was almost touching, then quick as a dart, clapped it over the piglet, tipped it up, closed the lid and tied it fast.

There were loud cheers from the onlookers, as, clutching my prize, I struggled out backwards to my feet. Someone shoved a flask of ale into my hands and, keeping tight hold of my basket, I swallowed deeply. A girl pushed her way to the front and held out her hands for the pig. I passed over the basket. She started to untie the lid, but I held it shut and shook my head. 'Take it and welcome,' I said. She gave me a smile.

I turned to accept the offer of more ale, then when I turned back, my basket was being pushed back at me. By one of Cedd's men.

'Cedd!' he called over his shoulder, pressing the basket into my chest. The youth was stocky and strong, but I took him on and held my ground, so that we were pushing the basket between us, in a trial of strength. I flicked a glance to where Cedd stood next to a hawk, touching its feathers, gently, with one fingertip.

'Cedd!' shouted the youth. 'Now's your chance!' Ale made him loose-limbed and he staggered, leering round at the crowd to see who was listening. I held on, jerking him upright to look at me. 'Show her whose land this is! Show her. Show her who's leader here! Cedd!'

Cedd looked up, then strode towards us. I gave the basket one last shove and the youth fell back, at the feet of others of Cedd's band. Helga and Leif now stood at my shoulder, hands on knives. I waved them back.

'*Waes thu hael*,' I said to Cedd, using the Saxon tongue. Cedd's face was impassive and he remained silent, his eyes fixed on mine. I made a fist, pressed it to my chest and bowed my head to him. 'Albinus has told me of the deaths of your parents and brothers, at the hands of Vikings. Before all this company, in the name of my people,' I said, 'I forgive you the beating—' some in the crowd sighed—'and acknowledge that debt.'

'Yes!' butted in the stocky youth. 'And you'll pay with your own blood, Viking—won't she, Cedd?' The stocky youth fumbled with a knife in his belt.

'That's enough! Ho, there! Clear the way!'

A tall monk appeared and shooed away the crowd. Behind him Albinus approached and put his hand on Cedd's shoulder. Encouraged by Albi's presence, I spoke again to Cedd. 'Tell me what recompense I can make,' I said. 'I will pay whatever I can, poor though it may be, for what true recompense can be made for such deaths?' My voice faltered, caught by the memory of my own loss, the death of my father, Thorkil. I was trying to find more words, more promises, when Cedd twisted away from Albi's grip.

'I know my duty,' he said, with an angry glance at Albinus. 'I don't need to be reminded of it.' He turned back to me. 'We're going hunting tonight, at sundown. Hares in the top acre. You need food? You should come. It's good hunting.'

Albinus looked relieved that Cedd had made me this offer, but I saw the bleak look in Cedd's eyes. Was the offer a trap?

Asa appeared at my side, but Cedd looked only at me, chin jutted, waiting for my answer, his arms folded across a short bow which he held tight to his chest. He tilted his shaven head, silently repeating his invitation. What should I do? Albi gave me a barely perceptible nod. I looked back at Cedd. 'Sundown then,' I said.

CHAPTER 7
CEDD

After supper, with the heat leaving the day, I dressed myself for the hunt. I cleaned my face and hands and put on my best tunic. I armed myself with sword and axe—I would not end as Cedd's quarry, whatever he had in mind—but I would not be the first to draw weapons. I would use them only to defend myself. Cedd would have to draw on me first.

Next I picked up my hunting gear: a pouch for the kill and a small bag full of meat—mice and bird—with which to entice Raed back to my arm.

'Bring back a hare! Bring back two!' Asa called as I left the shelter and she came to the doorway and stood watching as I mounted my pony and trotted away to collect Raed from Skar's pens. Skar questioned me with a look, too, as he settled Raed on to my shoulder.

'I'll be back before dark,' I said, 'with, Othinn willing, a fat hare or two.' Skar signed that he would come with me, and turned to untie his horse. I patted his shoulder.

'I shall go alone,' I said, and, with a shrug, Skar let me pass. A heavy chill cooled my spirits as I crossed the river to the Saxon side. Was I a fool to meet Cedd alone? Was it a trap? Should I go back for Skar? Raed shifted uneasily on my shoulder as I entered the wood. The light faded. I must set her to hunting before nightfall. There was no time to go back.

As I left the wood, taking a path that skirted the village, sheep snickered from the fields, to my left hand. It was the only sound. There was no one about, and, to my right hand, only faint trails of smoke from the hearthfires of the hovels to show that there were people there. To comfort myself with the sound of my own voice, I murmured to Raed, who now sat quiet on my shoulder as if she knew it was not time to worry yet.

Ahead of me, the top acre field glittered with frost. When I reached the wattle gate marking the entrance, I took Raed from my shoulder on to my arm and slipped from my pony, tying her to the low branch of a tree. There was no sign of Cedd.

I shifted the gate and walked into the field, breaking the icy crust in the furrows with loud cracks, and made for the corner furthest from the gate, where I had a clear view of wood and village. When Cedd arrived I would see him approach and so judge his intentions. Stroking Raed's chest, I settled down to wait.

Zing! A dart flew past my head and thwacked into the ground behind me. *Zing!* Another. With a prayer, I set Raed free and threw her into the sky, then threw myself to the ground. *Zing!* Another dart. *Zing!* Another. As the next dart hit the ground next to me, I realized that this was a warning. *Watch your step, Viking.* Cedd was not trying to kill me. Saxon bowmen, from childhood, are too skilled to keep missing their aim.

I stood up and, arms wide, walked out into the open. Cedd and his men emerged from their hiding places round the edge of the field, and stood to face me in a half circle at a distance of thirty or forty paces. *'Waes thu hael!'* I called out. 'Why such a fierce welcome? I'm here to hunt meat, with your consent, not to continue the war.' I took off my weapons. I slipped the sword and axe from my belt, held them high, then dropped them at my feet. There were shouts of 'Get her, Cedd!','Kill the Viking scum!','Finish her!'

'No!' Cedd shouted, turning to face them. Surprised, I listened to Cedd face down his own men. 'Her death will not bring back the dead! I will not have her blood on my hands! When she came as a thief in the night to hunt meat in our territory, *then* she was fair game for us. We drove her off, we defeated her and gave her a beating on the Hill. It's *enough. They—*' he pointed back at me, over his shoulder, '—are not going to go away! Do you want to bring the bloodlust of the raiders down on us again? If I can speak to her, I who lost mother, father, brothers to Viking swords, so can you. Father Anselm thinks we would be fools not to make peace with them!'

Watching Cedd was like watching myself. As leaders of our respective people, we had much in common. It is a difficult task sometimes, to argue your case and look to the good of the tribe, not to your own desires.

In answer to his words, some of the band instantly put away their weapons. Others shuffled uneasily, feathers in the wind, waiting for someone to lead them and make the decision about which way to blow. One, whom I named Bull-thighs, spat his contempt on to the ground. Cedd turned back to face me. 'There is still a payment to make,' he called out loud for all to hear. 'I claim wer-gild for the deaths of my parents and brothers, and for all deaths here that lie on the hands of your people.'

'I will pay for their deaths,' I replied, recognizing the time-honoured bargain between perpetrator and victim, for payment of blood debt, laid down by our common laws. 'I will pay all your wer-gild!'

'Huh!' shouted Bull-thighs. 'You shame your blood, Cedd, to settle with the enemy! Fight her, Cedd! Or show yourself to be a coward and let me fight her!'

'*Fight! Fight! Fight!*' An arrow zinged between us as the shouts broke out, as Bull-thighs egged on the others. Cedd swung round to address them.

'I am no coward! I shall fight the Viking! We shall fight, now, hand to hand! But afterwards—' he paused, waiting until he had all their attention, '—whatever the outcome, as your leader, I tell you there will be no more fights! No more bloodshed!' He looked back to me. 'Will you fight on those terms?'

'I will!' I shouted. 'But—I shall not be your quarry again!'

Amid much muttering, Cedd dropped his weapons and signalled to his men to stand back. As he hunkered down into a wrestling stance, they slapped their open hands on their thighs. 'Begga begga begga,' they chanted as if to call up a demon, and I admit I quailed at the sound, as they intended me to. 'Begga begga begga.'

I steeled myself. I would not let them put fear into my mind. Battles can be lost that way, without a blow being dealt. 'Come on, then,' I called, trying to keep my voice steady. 'Guard yourself.'

As Cedd and I circled each other, I stared into his clear blue eyes. *I'm faster*, I thought, *but he's stronger*.

Cedd leapt for me and I fell. I thought my jaw would break as he pushed his open hand under my chin, pressing my skull hard into the ground. I brought up my knee, thrusting my foot hard into his groin. Trying to throw him off was like trying to dislodge a sack of wet meal, but I rolled him over, then we clung together, before, with a mighty shove, I managed to push him away.

We took up the stance again, then I grabbed his arm and attempted to twist it. He took hold of my shoulder. The look in his eyes never faltered. *Strong arms, strong mind*. As if in a drunken dance, we spun round. I could not find his weakness.

Slowly, surely, he bent back my arm until the joint cracked. I drew breath and made my whole body seem boneless, lying limp in his hands. Then, before he had time to take tight hold, I slipped sideways, jumped up and away.

As I prepared to take up the stance again, Cedd grabbed me head-on, laid his hands on my shoulders and shoved me down to the ground. As he pinned me down, I had little room for manoeuvre, but there's always room for a trick. 'Albinus!' I shouted, darting a look over Cedd's shoulder, as if Albinus was standing there. It was enough to loosen Cedd's grip. Like a gift from great Othinn, came the sound of homecall, the sound of a horn; not Albinus's great trumpet, but a hunting horn like the ones used in the Mark. I stood up. A party of monks rode along the bottom of the field, on their way back to the monastery. 'Homecall, Cedd,' one shouted.

'I heard it, Brother Lucius,' Cedd replied. As Cedd's men turned to leave and made their way down the field to the wattle gate, I spotted Raed circling above the moorland that lay to the west of top acre. She took stand, then as she started her plunge to the prey, a dart knocked her from the sky.

I watched her spiral, the dart locked in her wing. Eyes narrowed, I swung round to see who had fired. Bull-thighs was lowering his bow. I roared, but Cedd reached him before me, grabbed the bow, then, with a great blow of his fist, knocked him to the ground.

Cedd's eyes never left me as his men ran from the field. As I turned, to see where on the moor Raed had fallen, Cedd bent to help Bull-thighs to his feet, before he too, supporting his warrior, left the field.

CHAPTER 8
MESSENGERS

There was no sign of Raed, though I searched on the moor until I could search no more. Bone-weary and heart-sore, I knelt on the soil and, Othinn forgive me, I wept like a child. My spirit grieved for my hawk; then, as if her loss had unlocked another grief, I wept for Thorkil and for all I had lost in the Mark. As the cold stars watched, I howled out all my tears until there were none left.

A small noise startled me and I got to my feet, wiping my face on the back of my sleeve. Something trotted towards me across the moor. The dog fox came within arm's reach and sat in front of me, its golden eyes fixed on mine. 'Why are you here?' I whispered. 'Has Othinn sent you to comfort me?' When I held out my hand, the fox licked at my fingers before trotting off, back across the moor.

Was the fox a messenger from the gods? Asa, who knew about such things, might be able to tell me.

The next day, at firstlight, I faced Asa across the hearth and took from her my bowl of oatmeal, warmed with a little hot water. The amount was pitifully small, but I smiled and thanked her, hoping to be forgiven for having returned from 'hunting' with Cedd with bruises on my face, but no meat. I had told her about Raed, but her bluff counsel was as I guessed it would be—'*Thank Othinn you were safe. There are plenty more hawks.*'

As I put down my empty bowl, Asa picked up a jar of salve to tend the grazes on my back from Cedd's beating, and came round to my side of the fire. I took off my shirt and leaned forward, hands clasped, elbows on knees, staring into the flames, while she salved the wound.

'I couldn't find Raed's body,' I said. 'I'm not sure that she's dead.' As if about to upbraid me for wasting time on what could not be mended, Asa gave a great sigh and rubbed hard at my back. 'Perhaps a wolf took her,' she said.

'I saw no wolf. I saw a fox. I have seen this same fox three times now.' Asa's fingers jabbed me so hard that I yelped.

'Where?' she said. 'Where have you seen this fox?'

'I told you at the market. I asked you if you saw it there, remember? The last time was on the moor, to the west of top acre,' I said.

Asa rubbed her hands clean. 'Put your shirt on.' She sat down next to me by the fire and stared into my eyes. 'Tell me about this fox,' she said.

After I'd finished speaking, Asa looked into the flames. 'Was it the same fox each time?'

'I'm sure it was. It had a forked patch on its nose.'

My stepmother touched the silver hammer of Thor she wore round her neck.

'It came to me and licked my fingers,' I said. 'Perhaps the fox brought me a message from Othinn.' I gave a nervous laugh. 'The gods are such riddlers.'

Asa went to the cedar chest she had brought from the Mark, which she had lodged in a corner of the shelter. Rifling through the contents, she threw out on to the floor all the rich clothes, soft shoes, fine leather belts, that belonged to the past. Finally she held up a hoop of twisted gold, a torc that my father had given her on their wedding day. I'd forgotten about it. Firelight blazed up and danced on the two animal heads that ornamented it, one at each end, designed to face each other on the wearer's throat. Fox heads.

'The fox does not come from Othinn.' Asa spoke the last words in a hoarse whisper, glancing round to see who might be watching from the shadows. 'I have seen the same fox.' My heart leapt like a hare under the hawk's shadow.

'You think that the fox comes from my father,' I said.

'It is his sign,' Asa said in a flat voice.

I stared at the torc, and the foxheads blurred as tears sprang to my eyes. *Fox. My father, the cunning one. Thorkil Redbeard.* My chest was tight as a pulled bowstring, as I whispered the unthinkable question.

'Does it mean he's alive?'

'No.' Asa shook her head. 'No, Thorkil died in the Mark—you know that. Your father's dead.'

Of course he was. His deathboat, burning, had rocked on the sea like a lantern, lighting his way to Valhal. My eyes had hurt with the watching, as I had followed the tiny black ruin of the ship until it was a dot on the horizon.

'Oh—' A low cry broke from her as if she was in pain. Asa gripped the front of her robe with her hands, pressing the torc to her chest. She pursed her lips and gave a fierce shake of her head, then she hugged herself and turned away so that she stood with her back to me, shoulders hunched. 'Oh—' That cry again.

Ice-cold, I pulled her to face me.

'What do you know? What does it mean?' Asa pulled away from me. 'Why does my father send me this sign? He died in battle,' I said, stubbornly clinging to what I believed to be true. 'He died with honour, with his sword in his hand, facing his enemy.'

Asa didn't speak and her shoulders trembled as she wept. 'Why do you link the fox with my father's death?'

The words Asa did not want to speak fell into my ears like molten lead. *The fox is a messenger from the dead—a fylgia—a shadow soul sent by a warrior who seeks vengeance. It is a sign of treachery. Betrayal. Murder.*

I pulled Asa round to face me, gripped her arms and shouted into her face. 'Why is my father's spirit not at rest?'

Shaking, Asa pushed me away. Then, holding the precious torc to her breast, as if it were a shield, she said: 'I don't know. I don't know.' She put her hand to the side of her head as if to still an ache. Her face drained of colour.

'What do you know?'

'Nothing. I swear it.' She put her hand on my arm but I wrenched it away. 'Beren. Listen to me. Make certain. We have to be certain. Watch for the fox. Tell me if you see it again.'

I didn't listen. I couldn't stay. I swept out of the shelter and ran into the wood. Asa came after me.

'You must ask Vasser's man, Grymma. He stood next to Thorkil when he was killed. He must have seen exactly what happened. Here—' she pushed a sack of meal into my arms. 'Take this to him. Speak to Grymma.' Grymma, Vasser's man, had stayed on the strand to look after the boats. Tyr, my father's warrior, was with him.

With my thoughts full of stings, I fixed a bridle on my pony and threw the sack over her back, hitting it smartly in the middle so that the weight fell evenly on either side. I mounted my steed, then pulled the reins round to head down the seaward path through the wood.

As I left the settlement, I went over the day of my father's death examining every detail.

That last day of battle I had spent fighting for my life on the beach, pushed ever backwards by the enemy, invaders who knew the value of the Mark and its trade routes to the east.

I didn't see Thorkil die. In the first attack, we were separated and I never saw him alive again. Herded together, our backs to the sea, I thought to make a last stand, when the cry went up—'The king is dead!'

I went over every detail. Vasser's men arranged his body, covering him with his fine green cloak, placing his sword and axe by his side, straightening his royal diadem. Then on my mark, we let loose the darts that set fire to the ship, and, when it was well ablaze, watched it plunge into the icy current.

I had not seen my father die. Vasser said that he had been killed in combat, hand to hand with the enemy chieftain. The fox, if it were a *fylgia*, told things differently. That my father had died shamefully. That his spirit was not in Valhal. That it cried out for vengeance.

I wanted to shake out the truth. I wanted to pull everything out into the clear light of day. Vasser. What did Vasser know?

In the silent, sunlit wood, my body crawled as if I were in danger, but there was not the slightest hint of it, as the sun shone, as it always does, on harm and innocence alike.

CHAPTER 9
VASSER'S MAN

We came from the Mark in two boats, large traders with deep holds where we stowed all we could carry: thirty-two souls in all, men, women, and children, six horses, four goats, and every one of Skar's hawks in their cages. Tyr, Thorkil's man, had charge of *Waverider*, the older vessel. I had charge of *Ravenseye*, smaller, but newer, with its fresh-hewn oarports and fine red and white sail.

Vasser came after us, in his *Wolfbane*, with his small fleet of warships that he and his men had now taken south to the war.

As I left the wood and rode down to the strand, Tyr ducked out from under the rim of *Ravenseye*, which, like *Waverider* next to it, lay upturned as a shelter, the gunwale propped up on the oars.

I looked for Grymma. Vasser's chief jarl had sustained a deep wound to his right shoulder and had stayed behind when Vasser left. I had asked him to join us, but he had chosen to remain on the strand, to guard the boats, with Tyr tending his wound.

'*Vestu hal*, Grymma!' I called. He did not reply, and as I rode towards Tyr, taking the sack of meal to the boat, he stayed at his post, halfway between shelter and sea,

✛ 67 ✛

as fixed as a rock. This did not bode well. As his queen I was due at least some sign of his respect. I did not expect a wounded man to stand but he should have answered my greeting.

'All well?' I asked Tyr as I dismounted.

'All well,' he repeated, taking the rein from me and tying Snorri to an oar port.

Tyr examined the meal for maggots. When he grunted his satisfaction and emptied the meal into a barrel, I said, 'How's Grymma today?'

'The same. His wound is the same, though I bathe it in brine every day.' He tapped the lid back on the barrel. 'Grymma's spirit is sore: he longs to join Vasser. This time of rest is irksome to him. His mind tells him that he will never be well. And so,' he said, folding the meal sack, 'his wound stays the same.'

Resting one hand on the gunwale, I looked out at Grymma's stubborn figure, then went to speak to him. '*Tu hal!*' I repeated my greeting, as I approached. Again he chose not to reply.

Grymma sat, still fully armed in his war gear, his long white hair covered by his iron helmet, in soiled mail shirt and jerkin, his legs in tough hide breeks. The head of his axe glinted from the top of his belt, the haft of a spear rested on his left shoulder. His eyes stayed fixed on the waves. His right arm, tied across his left shoulder, was bound with a bloodstained rag. His left hand splayed out on the rock at his side, warmed by the sun.

'Grymma.' I came round to face him and hunkered down so that our eyes were at a level. Finally he turned his eyes from the sea. His grim, weathered face, marked with tattoos, swirling patterns, blue scars, circles within circles, could terrify his enemy in battle, but now the patterns showed dark against a sickly pallor. I was shocked to see how his eyes flickered, like an old man's.

'Tyr! Bring some ale!' I called, but when Tyr offered the cup, Grymma waved it away.

'Why are you here, Thorkil's daughter?' he said, at last. Stung by his insolent words, I stood up.

'I am no longer anyone's daughter, Grymma. My father, Thorkil King, is dead. I am Berengeria Queen, and in Vasser's absence, you are subject to me. I demand your loyalty.' Grymma turned to look fixedly at the horizon.

'You cannot demand it,' he said, in a low voice. 'You will *command* it and I will give it freely—when I see a reason to change my allegiance. You will not be queen because your father Thorkil willed it so. You will be queen when you have proved yourself capable of holding men's lives in your hands.' With a great effort, Grymma hauled himself to his feet, and leaned heavily on his spear. 'When Vasser returns he will challenge you for the crown. Will you fight him for it?'

He did not wait for my answer, but turned his back on me and began to limp back to *Ravenseye*.

'What do you know of Thorkil's death?' I shouted.

For a breath Grymma stopped, but then went on again, so I drew my axe and threw it and it sang, like a silver turning wheel, past Grymma's shoulder and planted itself in the sand ahead of him. He stopped.

'You will tell me what you know!' I said, drawing my knife.

Grymma threw down his spear and, confronting me, held his left arm out wide. He could barely stand. 'Use your weapon,' he said. 'Kill me. I shall not resist.' My hand jerked forward, stabbing the air. Grymma did not falter, but put his head back to take the blow.

I sheathed my blade. 'I was wrong to threaten you. You deserve better and I deserve the truth. What do you know of Thorkil's death?'

'He died a hero's death,' said Grymma. I picked up his spear and handed it to him.

'I have seen a sign,' I said. 'Thorkil's sign. The fox. It is a shadow soul—a *fylgia*—Asa thinks so. It comes from my father, Thorkil. It speaks of treachery. Tell me what you know.'

Grymma's face closed against me. He looked over my shoulder at the sea. 'Thorkil died a warrior's death, face to face with his enemy, sword in hand.' The words were an empty repetition, as if he had studied what to say if he were ever questioned. Then he turned and continued back to the shelter.

'Whom do you serve?' I called. Again I confronted him. 'Did you see Thorkil die? Tell me the truth!'

Swaying, Grymma remained silent. Finally I tried a bowshot in the dark. 'We have only Vasser's word for what happened. He told us how Thorkil died. My uncle Vasser. It is his word. Can we believe what we've been told? Were you there? What did you see?' Grymma's lips narrowed, but remained closed.

'The time will come,' I said, 'when you must choose whom to follow. If Vasser challenges me, I shall fight him. I shall lead this tribe, not as Vasser's mate nor as his chattel. There will be no queen—that title is meaningless here—but I shall lead the tribe. We can't survive on our own. We must settle things with the Saxons and find a way of living in peace.'

Grymma grunted with scorn. 'Why bother to settle things? When Vasser returns he will wipe these Saxons from the face of the earth.'

'Not with my help. I will not put my hand to unprovoked slaughter. We shall sheathe our weapons, and give up waging war. We're a new people now, Grymma, in a new land. We'll share it with the Saxons, together. They know this land—we can learn from them.'

'Learn from *Saxons*? Live with *Saxons*?' Grymma looked away, as if he could not believe his ears. When he looked back at me, his face was twisted with disgust. Then he spat at my feet. 'Your mother was Saxon. I shall not follow a half-bred.'

Again my hand sprang to my knife. 'Then you will leave this place,' I said.

'Vasser is my master,' Grymma said. 'I take my orders from him.'

As he turned to leave, his left leg gave way and he fell. I longed to help him, to spring forward and put my arm under his, but I knew he would interpret such action as weakness. In the end, Tyr carried him back to the boat.

'Grymma, we shall speak again,' I said, reaching the boat. Tyr handed me the empty meal sack and I stowed it in my pack.

As I unhooked Snorri's rein, Tyr said, 'I can do nothing more for the wound. The sickness spreads. Grymma is a fine warrior. If he dies, he will live for ever in Valhal.'

'Not with my father. Not with Thorkil.' The words dropped like stones from my lips. 'His spirit is not at rest.' I mounted my pony and took up the rein. 'If Grymma speaks of Thorkil or Vasser, take note. He knows more than he's saying.'

As I tugged Snorri's rein, Tyr caught my hand.

'Grymma is Vasser's man—but I am Berengeria's. At risk of death, I shall tell you what I know. I can't join you yet—I won't leave Grymma to die alone—old loyalties—' Slightly shamed, Tyr tilted his head. 'But I shall come to the camp, soon, for fresh water. Then I shall speak—for the debt I owe to your father—Othinn protect us all.' He pressed something into my hand, closing his fingers tight over mine to make a double fist, then, with a sharp nod, ducked back inside the boat.

I opened my hand. Inside was a gold ring, carved with the head of a fox, Thorkil's gift to his most valued warrior.

CHAPTER 10
HIDDEN ENEMIES?

'*I shall tell you what I know.*' Tyr's words sat heavily in my mind. There was something to tell then. It was the first real evidence I had of some—for want of a better word—some *mishap* to do with my father's death. How could I bear waiting for Tyr to speak?

I could go back to the strand. I could go back now and demand that Tyr give me his witness, but if I did, he would betray to Grymma his true loyalties, which might place his life in danger.

Locked in thought, I sat, until Snorri shifted her hooves, startled by a raven's croak. There was nothing I could do to force this issue. I tugged at the rein and rode hard back to the camp. Much better to wait. Better to let Tyr speak when he judged it safe to do so.

Grymma's open defiance had shaken me. Who could I trust? When Vasser returned, how many of the tribe would turn their backs on Thorkil's daughter and swear their blades to him?

Thirty-one souls lived in my care, and I had never thought to question their loyalty. If I went against Vasser, would they follow me? No leader fights alone. If the fates brought me face to face with my uncle, who would stand with me?

Slowing Snorri to a walk, I took out Tyr's ring and smoothed the gold with my fingertip. I could count on Tyr. I could count on Asa, Helga and Skar, Brand and Brokk. What of Arn and Finn? What of Leif Ropemaker? What of the rest?

There was a simple way to answer my questions. I would hold moot, a gathering where we could take time to talk to each other, about simple ordinary things, everyday things, such as the food supplies and making more shelters, finding a way to share tools and tasks, preparing to trade, deciding what dealings we should have with the Saxons. In this way I should find out the tribe's opinion of me. I would find a way to broach the subject of Vasser's return and I would let them know that, if necessary, I would fight him for the crown. Then, I would put it to the vote. Who would you have as leader? Vasser Wulf? Or Beren Thorkilsdatter? Then, if my people chose Vasser, I would leave and never return. How often had Thorkil said, *'Let the people decide. No one can lead if the people will not follow.'*

As I entered the deep part of the wood, my eyes flicked to the shadows. Something stirred. I drew rein and waited. *The fox?* Not this time. When the hooded man showed himself, silhouetted in a gap between the trees, I reached for my bow and nocked a dart. The figure stayed within range: I could have killed him.

'Who are you?' I called, as the figure threw his cloak over his shoulder. There was a long jagged tear in the cloth. *I shall know you again*, I thought. He made no move against me, but slid between the trees, keeping his distance. 'Answer me or I'll fire!' I called. I sighted along the dart, then, as I drew back the bowstring, he disappeared. I stood up in my footholds, but could see no sign of him.

'Speak to me!' I called. For answer there was only the steady drip drip of rain from the branches. Sometimes the gods tease us for their amusement. 'Othinn! Great Othinn! Show yourself! I'm not afraid!' I called, though my voice shook. 'How did Thorkil die?' I asked. 'Show me!' Then, with a great shout: 'Where is my uncle, Vasser?'

Man, spirit, great Othinn: all were implacably silent. I spurred Snorri back to the camp.

Asa met me at the dense barrier of thorn, at the western end of the camp. 'What did you learn?'

Dismounting I shook my head and called to Brand, who stood on guard. 'Did you see him? A hooded man? On foot, carrying a staff?'

Brand shook his head, then shouting Leif to accompany him, mounted his pony. 'We'll search the wood,' he said.

I walked back with Asa to the shelter.

'Grymma will say nothing about Thorkil's death, except what we were told—and what I believe he was *told* to say if questioned—that Thorkil died facing the enemy, with his sword in his hand.'

Asa gathered the folds of her tunic and sat beside me.

'One thing is clear,' I said. 'Grymma is Vasser's man. If Vasser challenges me for the crown, Grymma will fight for him.' I gripped Asa's hands. 'How many others will do the same? Vasser is a strong warrior. If it came to a choice, won't they choose him?'

Asa put her hand on my shoulder. 'Thorkil chose you. No one else. You are queen.' Ashamed of my moment of weakness, I stood up to escape the comforting touch of her hand.

'Today we hold moot. Gather everyone together.'

Later, when I entered the shelter, the sour smell of woodsmoke and goat made me smile. Helga was there, but no one else. She looked up from her sewing, a piece of torn sail spread across her ample lap.

'Where's Asa?' I said.

'Skar took her off to the hawk pens,' Helga replied. Her old red face wrinkled with glee. We both spluttered into a giggle. It was no secret that Skar was in love with my stepmother. Asa was not yet ready to seek another mate, but she still spent time with him, determined to be friends, if nothing more.

'Has she told you about the moot?'

'Yes. It's about time,' Helga said, biting off her thread. 'We've all been waiting for you to say the word.'

That same day, with Brokk reporting no sight nor sound, hide nor hair of our mysterious watcher, we all gathered for first moot and the shelter, like the finest ale hall, clamoured with the sound of people talking and clinking their cups, jostling and joking.

As soon as Asa returned from her own moot with lovelorn Skar, she had thrown herself into preparations: there was bread and some goats' cheese, traded from the Saxons, and a cask of their ale which I had bartered myself for a fine gold armring. It was little to pay, after all, to see people smiling again.

When all had gathered, I went to stand on a large flat stone, set as a dais at one end of the shelter. '*Vestu hal!*' I called. '*Vestu hal!* All hail and welcome!' I raised my cup in a toast: 'To safe harbour and a full belly!'

'To safe harbour . . . and a full belly!' they replied and the roar of voices filled the shelter. I drank deep, then waited while Asa took the ale-horn to each one of the company, until all had a taste of the ale. As the last drop was taken, I held high the silver moot-horn and called the company to attention. When all fell silent, I began to speak.

'You know that my father Thorkil willed me his crown. And I would be your queen—or if not *queen*, because who can be a queen without land . . . ?' I paused briefly, as a murmur of agreement rippled through the company. 'Thorkil taught me well and I hope I have proved myself sufficient, though we live in difficult times, with many and various *difficulties* . . . ' Their attention ebbed with this poor start, and some started to mutter. Then I saw Tyr at the back of the crowd. Was he ready to speak what he knew? He gave a brief nod as if I had asked the question out loud, and, as he came forward, I held up my hands, calling again for the people to hear me.

'There is something I have to tell you—' I said, above the current of mutters, '—about my father's death. Thorkil's *death*—' I called, and the company fell still. 'I believe . . . I *know* . . . there is more to discover.' Uproar followed. Calming the noise, I called out, 'There are questions to ask!' I gestured to my remaining hearth companions to join me on the dais. Asa and Brand made to draw swords, but I told them to sheathe their blades. Now silent, the people stared up at us. They knew what it meant: that their loyalty was being brought into question.

Tyr climbed on to the dais and took up the horn. 'Tyr has something to tell,' I said, stepping back.

'All hail!' Tyr greeted the company and they replied to his greeting. 'I have one thing to tell—' he began, '—about the day Thorkil died. It has grieved me, this one thing that I know and it will be a heavy burden set down, a soul-easing, to speak of it.'

'Then speak!' was the cry from several voices.

Tyr nodded, then turned to me: 'Before you ask, I did not see Thorkil die. No. I heard only the words of Lord Vasser, that Thorkil died facing his enemy with his sword in his hand—' He paused and looked at the faces ranged below him. 'First let me say this—that I was Thorkil's man, and I swear now, before you all, that until the day of my death, I am Berengeria's.' The silence in the shelter was complete. 'I ask you now to consider whom to choose as your leader. Whom to trust. You may have to choose, when Vasser returns. Now I shall tell what I saw on the day Thorkil died. Hear me.

'The fighting in my part of the field was fierce and relentless. We were outnumbered from the beginning, the enemy pouring over our defences like floodwater. I and my companions were soon separated from Thorkil. We tried but we could not reach him and when I saw that Vasser himself, with his own band of jarls, had taken on the task of protecting the king, I turned my sword to other work.

'There was a pause in the fighting, as there is sometimes, when you least look for respite, and I again looked to the king. That's when I saw it—I saw Lord Vasser and the chief of the Jutlanders face to face. There was only a step between them, but they each lowered their swords.' Tyr's hand moved to echo the gesture. 'No blow was struck. They looked at each other, then they passed each other by, going on to kill other men.'

Tyr brushed his hand over his eyes, as a murmur of shock spread though the company. 'It was a moment only, but I know what I saw. Lord Vasser had the life of the enemy chieftain in his hand—like this—' Tyr held up his clenched fist and slowly twisted it, 'and he let him go.'

As the murmur of the crowd grew to an angry muttering, I too held up my hand for silence. I stepped to Tyr's side.

'This I fear,' I began, 'that the spirit of Thorkil Redbeard does not lie content in Valhal. I have reason to suspect treachery. I have reason to question my uncle Vasser. I will have the truth.' I paused and looked round the assembly. 'If Vasser proves guilty of treachery, he shall be brought to account.'

'If Berengeria Queen sets herself against Vasser Wulf, who will stand with her?' Tyr called. Once more silence greeted his words. He raised his fist and shook it over his head. 'You must choose! Choose now! Who will stand with Beren Queen?'

Silence. My heart quailed. Then, in answer to his simple question came a single voice, then a shout of voices, in a roar of sound to lift the sailroof into the night.

'For Berengeria! For Beren Queen! All hail Thorkil's daughter! All hail! All hail! All hail!'

Tears stood in my eyes as the sound of the 'all hail' went on and on, until Tyr held up his hand for silence. Many had drawn their blades. 'Hold hard,' I cried. 'We shall not use swords until we have to. Before I raise a weapon against my father-brother, I must have proof.'

'Where will you find such proof?' someone shouted from the crowd. 'Do you go back to the Mark?'

I considered telling them about the fox, but I held my peace. My 'sightings' seemed too tenuous to be evidence of treachery. If the fox were indeed a messenger, its message was not yet clear.

'I shall not go back to the Mark. We must be patient and wait for Vasser's return. When he knows my suspicions he will not be able to hide the truth. Meanwhile we must prepare for one last battle. If my uncle proves traitor, he shall pay for his crime.'

With a nod to Asa, I raised my cup again. 'For Thorkil. Rest and honour in Valhal!' Others echoed the toast. Having drunk, I said only: 'I promise you, we shall have answers,' then I stepped down from the stone. 'Meanwhile, we shall have games!' I led them out of the shelter.

On a patch of cleared ground where Brokk and Brand conducted daily weapons drill, we gathered for our games. It was late in the afternoon, the light and heat of the day on an ebbtide, and many collected to warm themselves in the glow of Brokk's forge, on the edge of the clearing. Talk of treachery was soon lost in exchange of boasts and wagers, and I admit that, witnessing the joy of people sharing a simple pastime, I relaxed my guard. Cedd took us all by surprise.

CHAPTER II
CEDD'S VISIT

Struggling to take a firm hold on the ball Helga had made, from hide greased with pig fat, I was helpless with laughter. I had it—took aim—threw it—tossed it into the barrel—ran back to claim the hit by marking a notch on my stick—then froze as Brand moved to the thorn fence, his hand on the hilt of his blade. Cedd was there, sitting motionless astride his horse.

He must have been there for a while, watching from the trees; his rein was loose and his horse stood head-down, teasing the dry grass out from between tree roots with its big square teeth.

'State your purpose,' Brand said. I sensed rather than heard him bite back the word, '*Saxon.*'

'Your leader knows me. I must speak with her,' Cedd replied.

'There's no need for weapons,' I said. 'I know this man.'

As I came up to the barrier, Cedd dismounted and looped his rein to a branch. 'He's alone,' Brand whispered, as I passed. 'I'll take a look around anyway.' I nodded my agreement—there was no point in taking a risk—and he beckoned Leif to go with him.

Frowning, Cedd stood by the fence, making no move to enter the camp. He looked troubled, his blue eyes glaring at me from under his thick black brows. Why had he come? He wore no weapons, only the knife at his belt. There was a leather sack over his shoulder.

'*Waes thu hael!*' I said, using the Saxon greeting, pulling the thorn aside to let him pass. Alone, unarmed, he was welcome, yet I could not help briefly touching the hilt of my own blade—like everyone else I had put my weapons aside for the games—it was a habitual gesture, not meant to threaten Cedd. When I saw that he had noticed, I quickly dropped my hand to my belt.

As Cedd stepped into the camp, walking past me to take a long look about, the others stood in small groups at a distance, watching and waiting. I made furtive gestures for them to carry on with their doings and Brokk threw a log on the fire.

Sparks flew up in a cloud of smoke. There was the mouth-watering smell of roast pig. Sigrid again turned the spit. Helga picked up the greased ball and declared Arn the winner of the bannock. There were desultory cheers. Arn, our giant, held out his ham fist for the cake, then, with eyes wide, ate it whole. Still Cedd stood without speaking.

Asa brought us the ale-horn. '*Vestu hal,*' she said to Cedd, holding it out to him. Cedd ignored the ale, took the leather sack from his shoulder and laid it, I have to say, with great care, at my feet.

'What's this?' I said. I reached for the sack, and, as I did so, it moved.

I dropped to my knees and carefully released the hide thong that fastened the neck. Then I opened it wide, reached inside and drew out Raed's body. I stroked her feathers. Her eyes were closed, her beak slightly open. She was still warm. I felt Raed move: she was still alive.

I glanced up at Cedd, surprised that he had brought my hawk back to me. 'After we left the top acre, I watched you search the moor. I witnessed your grief and I was sorry for it. When you left, I took up the search myself and found the hawk. Such a beautiful creature should not have been felled by any dart, Saxon or Viking.' His face softened into the breath of a smile.

As Skar took Raed down to the pens, I held out my hand to Cedd. 'Thank you for bringing the hawk,' I said. He took my hand. I thought he was about to speak, when Brand rode round from the back of the shelter.

'Report,' I said.

'All well,' Brand said, shooting a glance of suspicion at Cedd, before dismounting and leading his horse away.

I turned back to Cedd. 'You have done a friend's turn here, but it may take time for my people to see it. Stay now, drink some ale with us. Break bread with us.'

When Brand returned, he took the knife from his belt and passed it to one of the others, then approached Cedd. 'What about wrestling? Will you wrestle, friend?'

Now Cedd spoke. He took hold of my arm. 'We have not finished our wrestling match. Will you finish it now?'

Hiding my surprise, I said: 'By all means!'

Inside a circle of torchlight, watched by the gleaming faces of my tribe, I set to wrestle with Cedd. We had both removed our knives and stripped off our outer tunics, and were both evenly matched for body size and weight. Hunkering down, opposite Cedd, I thought of the way we had fought on top acre. He was stronger. It would take all my cunning and guile to overcome him. As Asa dropped the cloth, the signal, Cedd leapt for me, his right fist closed, for a hammer blow. I ducked out of reach, and seizing his arm, just behind the fist, on the long bone, pushed him on and away, using his own force against himself. He sailed past me and landed on his chin on the ground. There was a cheer and Brokk put a stone in the pail. First fall to me.

I lost the next. Whirling to his feet, Cedd used his head as a butt to my ribs and I fell, with the wind blown from my sails. The stone went to Cedd's pail.

Taking breath, I considered my next move. My best. I walked over to where Cedd was hunkering into the stance. As he stood up to meet me, I gripped his wrists, applying all my strength to the hold. Thorkil taught me the move. It can weaken an opponent's sinews so that his hands tremble and hang limp as fine grass after-wards for up to a day.

When Cedd's eyes finally flickered and narrowed, I knew he had had enough. 'I have a strangler's grip,'

I said, letting go. He rubbed his wrists and acknow-
ledged the round to me. Brokk put the stone in my pail.

Thinking the bout was settled, I made the mistake of
turning my back on Cedd and found myself in a tight
headlock. He dragged me backwards to the circle
boundary. If I crossed it, he could claim the bout. I dug
my heels in the ground, pushing hard into him, so that
we both fell and lay, like beached fish, gasping, flat on
our backs.

'Water!' I called. I never learn. As I stood up and
turned my back, Cedd lazily reached over and chopped
the legs from under me with his strong right arm. I fell
like a toppled tree and the look of shock on my face
must have been very funny, because everyone laughed.

When Cedd sat up on one elbow and drew breath, I
scooped up a handful of mud from a puddle and threw
it at him. It covered his face and dripped off his chin.
Blinking mud from his eyes, he looked like a brown
owl, which set off more laughter. When we set to
again, others joined in, sparring, exchanging blows
and bangs, and the mood lightened, more festival than
fight.

Cedd and I knelt facing one another, propping each
other up with hands on each other's shoulders, weary
to the bone. Now we were more like friends than enemies.
When you are struggling hand to hand with your opponent, there is no room for deceit: your hands send the
messages. You soon know who wishes to kill you or
who is merely testing their strength against yours.
Cedd did not mean to harm me.

As I hauled him to his feet, there were smiles and cheers everywhere, for both of us. The bout was declared a draw. Cedd and I finished the night staring into the last embers of the fire, sharing the ale-horn.

'It was good wrestling,' I said, wiping ale foam from my mouth. He was about to reply—there was a smile on his face—when a dart hissed between us and plugged into the tree at our backs. I grabbed my knife and leapt to my feet, as Brand and others ran from the torchlit circle into the dark wood. They returned almost at once, accompanied by Grymma, fully armed and on horseback. On foot, behind him, Tyr stood.

'Thorkil's daughter!' Grymma replaced his bow over his shoulder and rode into the middle of our clearing. Still carrying my knife, I walked to the middle of the circle to face him.

'Speak, Grymma Jarl!'

Grymma drew his sword and pointed it at Cedd. 'Why do you soil yourself with such vermin? This land is Viking. They must be taught who is master. And not by a landless girl. Vasser is my leader, not Thorkil's daughter.' He raised his blade and shook it above his head, shouting in a voice to raise the birds from their roosts in the treetops: 'I am bloodsworn to the service of Vasser Wulf. At his side, in peacetime or war, I will live or die. I ride south to the war—come with me who will. I shall nursemaid it no longer, nor deal with you—any of you—' he swung his blade like a pointer along the circle of faces, 'who, like Tyr'—he spat at Tyr's feet—'have forgotten your blood right. When Vasser comes here, he will expect to find Vikings who *know* who they are.' He lowered his blade and pressed the point of it to my chest. 'He will rule here.'

I knocked his blade aside. With hatred blazing from his eyes, he slowly sheathed his sword in his belt, then gave a sharp tug to his rein and rode back into the wood. Behind me I heard my people pick up their weapons. I turned and shook my head. 'Let him go,' I said. 'It would take force or terror to change Grymma's loyalties. I do not rule by fear. That's not my way.'

Someone brushed roughly past me. Cedd strode towards the south boundary. He was leaving.

'Cedd!' When he turned back, I saw the blood welling from a wound in his cheek. He covered it with his fingers. Before I could stop him, Cedd had hauled himself on to his horse and was heading back to the river.

'I'll go after him,' said Brand.

'No,' I said. 'I will.'

CHAPTER 12
THE SAXON VILLAGE

It was days before I had the chance to seek out Cedd. Grymma's challenge had shaken us, as a high wind shakes the root of the rooftree, so I spent time calming the fretful mood in the camp, by giving my people the chance to bring their thoughts out into the open.

The talk that night, and the next day, when we held moot, was all of Vasser's return and the last battle that I had spoken of. In moot, we speak our minds and hold nothing back. Some spoke against such a battle. Finn, the miller, for one: 'How can we fight against Vasser and his jarls? Weary as they must be, worn down by the fighting with Guthrum, and most weary from the long journey home, we would be as candle flames to their wolves' breath. Soon dispatched.' He pinched finger and thumb together.

Another took up the moot-horn, holding it high to claim the attention of the company. It was Sigrid Ulfsdatter, next to youngest of the tribe, not yet blooded in battle. Her hand shook: she was fearful of speaking in front of the others, yet, driven by a worse fear, she took up the horn. When all were quiet, she stood gathering her words, and I studied her serious face, her long fair hair tied back as she entered her womanhood, and her wide blue eyes. When she finally spoke, the words burst from her heart: 'What if you die? What will happen to us?'

For a long breath I looked at Sigrid, keeping my eyes soft and kindly, because I knew that I must not show my own fear. Then I let my gaze travel over the faces and eyes of others. 'Only Great Othinn knows the day of my death,' I said lightly, 'yet I fear I shall live to bother you, Sigrid Ulfsdatter, with the quarrelsome demands of an old woman. I appoint you my keeper in old age. You shall tend me, wash me, feed me, and sing me to sleep. And practise your stories. I love bedtime stories.' I pointed my finger at her. 'Will you promise to do this?'

Sigrid hung her head, the corners of her mouth curled into a smile and she looked up at me. 'I promise,' she said. Laughter greeted this exchange.

When it died down a little, I lifted the horn. 'Great Othinn grant that I live to fight Vasser for my crown, because it was my father's wish that I lead this tribe. Thorkil gave me the crown. He did not give it to Vasser Wulf. Why he did not is a question that puzzles me, but he did not, and that is enough. I am queen and I will keep my crown. But Finn is right—' moving my gaze from Sigrid, I drew Finn's attention, 'we cannot stand alone against Vasser Wulf and his jarls, should he choose to fight. We must find allies, warriors who would come at our summons, to stand with us in time of need—'

At that, a confusion of talk broke out, then Arn said in his booming voice: 'We must go to King Halfdan.'

'King Halfdan's court—Jorvik—is several days' ride to the north,' I said. 'I have already considered whether to approach him. It is my true opinion that Halfdan will not send warriors to help us, nor any of the Viking leaders,' I said. 'This fight, if it comes to it, is a private matter, between Vasser and me, a family dispute. Halfdan will not intervene.'

'Then what do we do?' called Arn, spreading his huge hands.

I held my peace, waiting for someone else to come to the same lastword that I had. There was only one answer to Arn's question, only one last thing we could do.

'We ask help from the Saxons.' Brand. Faithful Brand. He stood with his arms across his chest, holding his upper arms tight, as if to protect himself from the very thought he had just uttered. There was a deep silence, into which I dropped my final words, as stones into a still pool. 'Tomorrow, I shall go to the Saxon monastery. I shall speak to the monks' leader, Father Anselm, lay all before him and ask for their help.'

When I put down the horn, there was silence. None offered to pick it up. When Asa passed round ale and breadcakes, the silence broke into muted discussion. Helga, Brand, Brook, and Arn stood in talk together. Sigrid and little Gerd broke bread with Finn and Geir, all nodding thoughtfully. The moot was not over, the discussions would continue, no doubt for many hours, but a decision had been made.

* * *

'You can't go alone,' Asa said. 'At least take Brand!' Full of disquiet, she fussed over me, handing me the blade she had just washed and polished. I put the knife in my belt. Before broaching the Saxon monastery, I would visit Cedd.

'To keep Cedd's trust, I must go alone,' I said. My loved stepmother clucked with disapproval, shaking her head, as she passed me the precious jar of honey salve, which I would offer Cedd to treat his wound. I tucked the jar safely inside my tunic.

Brand entered the tent.

'What is it?' I said, tightening my belt.

'This hidden man, the one watching the camp, I'd like another chance to flush him out.'

'Do so,' I said. 'Othinn grant you better luck!'

'Othinn defend you!' Brand said, as he left.

Asa passed me a large square of fine clean linen. 'A gift for Cedd's mother.' I shot her a glance and she immediately understood its meaning. *Cedd has no mother.* 'His grandmother then—or whoever there is to care for him.'

I shook my head—I was not sure there was anyone to look after Cedd—but I folded the linen carefully and pushed it into my belt. Gifts favouring the giver, it might ease my path.

I was ready to leave when Asa rummaged in her sack of possessions, pulled something out, polished it with a cloth, then held it out to me. 'Take this to the head of the monastery. Father Anselm, you say?' Asa placed a large silver cross in the palm of my hand. It was finely wrought, with a swirling pattern of gripping beasts, and, in the centre, a large shiny red garnet.

'It's beautiful,' I said, with the craven thought that it was too beautiful to send on what might be a fruitless quest.

Asa shrugged and sighed. 'Yes, it is beautiful, but more use as a gift to ease your path at the monastery than rotting away at the bottom of my sack.' I pushed the cross inside my tunic.

As I turned to leave, I smelt Asa's cedar oil and heard the scratch of her flint, as she lit a lamp to honour Othinn.

'Beren,' she said, 'before you go, grant me this favour. Before you cross the river, at least ask for Othinn's protection.'

We stood on opposite sides of the fire, and though I tried to still my mind to the ritual, I shuffled my feet through all Asa's prayers. I wanted to leave, to get on with my mission. Unarmed I must cross the river, the boundary between our two tribes, I must ride into the Saxon settlement. With every step, Saxon bowmen might take aim at me with their darts. Would they hold fire to listen? I longed to be done with the task.

But I knew better than to argue with my stepmother. Asa spends much time communing with the other-world: I find plenty to do in this one. She threw a few drops of ale on to the fire. 'Great Othinn, hear our prayer,' she said. 'Make clear your will to us. Drive away the doubts that stain our minds. Show us our true enemies.' Once more she threw herbs on the fire, which sent up a sudden dense cloud of fragrant smoke.

I could no longer see Asa. I was in the cave in the Hill and the fox sat in front of me. I tried to speak but my mouth was dumb. The fox climbed up the wall of the cave, leaping sure-footed from ledge to ledge. By the light of a torch, I followed its progress. As it reached the top ledge, just below the roof of the cave, I saw the flames flatten. There must be a stiff breeze. Then the fox disappeared.

'Beren!' Someone was holding me by the chin, shaking my face. 'Beren!' Asa bent over me and dripped cold water on to my lips. As I coughed and sat up, she passed me a beaker of cold water, which I swallowed with a gulp. 'Have you eaten today?'

I stared at her as if I had never seen her before. She repeated the question, then fetched a hunk of stale bread anyway. 'You can give up all ideas of crossing the river until you have food in your belly.'

When I tried to stand up, Asa laid her strong hand on my shoulder. 'Eat this,' she said. I took the bread.

In between bites, I asked: 'What happened? Did you see anything?'

'Did you?'

'I thought—oh.' I stood up and went to stand half in, half outside the shelter, with my hand gripping the hem of the sail-roof. Was the fox really a messenger from my father? Or had Asa's herbs triggered a memory? Something I'd seen in the cave and then forgotten? I couldn't remember an opening, or seeing the fox climb the wall, but I remembered the torch flame. It had lain flat in a strong draught. And I remembered hearing the sea. There had to be a gap, a gateway which led to the outside.

'You saw something, didn't you? What was it?' Asa asked.

I glanced round at my stepmother. Was it message or memory? Before I confided in Asa, I had to be sure. Secretly crossing my fingers, I said: 'Nothing, I saw nothing.'

Perhaps Asa believed me. She questioned me no further, then when I left she said: 'You will ask about trade? Show them the cross, get me some orders.' She turned to her workbench, picking things up and moving them, checking what items she had to offer. 'Tell them I'll barter silver for food—meal, grain, anything.'

'I'll try,' I said, wondering if I would have the chance for trade talks, and wondering at Asa's ability to live in the moment, pushing away all future fears. Is that what all mothers do? Riding out of the camp, I looked back, and there she was standing outside the shelter, bent over the bread trough and pummelling the dough, as if she were at home in the Mark.

There were no guards on the Saxon side of the ford, though with every step deeper into their territory I expected the Saxon wards to challenge me. None did. The place was deserted.

When I came to a bank and ditch, which must mark their line of first defence, I dismounted and tied Snorri to a thorn bush with plenty of haws left for her to pick at. Beyond the ditch, after a wide stretch of waste ground, there was a fence of sorts marking the village enclosure, though its row of drunken stakes, all at odds with each other, held together with clods of old wattle, was not worth the name. On the other side I could see some roofs and parts of shelters, broken, unkempt, stretching either side of an overgrown track.

I stood at the top of the ditch, took out my knife and held it high for any watcher to see, then I placed it on the ground. With my arms held wide, holding the salve, I called out in the Saxon tongue: 'I'm unarmed. I've come to see Cedd. I bring medicine for his wound.'

No one answered. No one moved. No one came to the broken fence. After waiting sufficient time for them to show themselves, I tucked the salve back inside my tunic and slithered down into the ditch, clambered up the other side, and walked towards the ruined fence.

As I carefully broke a way through it, I counted perhaps twenty huts scattered within its pale. Beyond the village, to the west, there were fields, now overgrown. To the east, an outreach of the wood, curving round the village, protecting it like a mother's arm. On the other side of that, I guessed, was the main north road, which led to the trading place, and, after it, Albinus's monastery. Crossing the road, due east, led to the Hill, and beyond that, the sea.

The roofs of the hovels were thatch, some fresh, it's true, this season's certainly, but half finished, as if done by a novice. Some had caved in already, the result of a storm perhaps, and stood unrepaired. Some were sensibly weighted with rope and stone, in the way we secured ours in the Mark, but again, the job was not well enough done, with frayed ropes or stones that were too light, so that the late winds had got under the thatch and blown it awry.

The village looked more like a camp, set up overnight for a party of warriors. Everywhere were the remains of the dwellings, piles of old withy and daub, scattered bowls, broken baskets and rags. I kicked a pile and smelt singed wood, scorched land. This village had been burnt. I shivered. Had Vikings done this? Where were the inhabitants? *Surely*—my mind veered away from the black thought that they had all been killed. *Burning villages . . .* I knew about the raids from the tales told in the Mark. But until I stood on this ruined ground I hadn't understood what it meant. *Killing farmers . . . innocent people, without weapons.*

I shivered, unable to believe that Vikings could do this. There must be a way to make the peace, but what could begin to repair this damage? This was a mighty blood debt which we had to find some way to pay.

I thought on more hopeful things. We were beginning to settle, we were beginning to trade. But would I ever really mend things with Cedd and his people?

Then, like vengeful ghosts, one by one, Cedd's men appeared and began to follow me. One carried kindling, but set it down as soon as he saw me. Another sat grinding a blade, then stood up and fell into step behind me, keeping a distance.

Pale-faced children appeared and sat at the edge of the track as I walked by, keeping watchful eyes on me, as they poked at small piles of pebbles or cradled their straw dolls. One had a pet jackdaw, which called out as I passed. 'Hwaet! Hwaet!' it called. 'Hwaet!'

'I'm looking for Cedd,' I said to the bird's companion, a thin child, her face marked with the round pits of an old disease. She stroked the bird and pointed to the very end of the track. Through narrowed eyes, I made out the grey shape of a hut, standing apart from the rest.

Cedd's home must once have been the most important dwelling in the village, the first call for visitors, standing on ward and watch. Now, it was tumble-down, a half-ruined hovel in a weedy patch of land. There was a large jagged hole in the thatch and one of the sides sagged out of true, the wattles bristling like the stubble of a giant's beard. The way in was covered by a dirty rag.

'I must speak to Cedd!' I called to those who still followed me. They stood and watched as I approached the hut.

Cedd!' I called and, after a pause, pulled the rag aside. The hut stank of decay and dirt, of something long dead, and I covered my nose against the stench.

It had once been a king's dwelling, that much was clear, with benches for the hearth companions lining the walls, and a board on a dais, now cobwebbed, cov-ered with a layer of dust. A Saxon helmet lay there and a swordbelt. A handful of weapons, now full of rust and grime, hung on the walls.

Cedd lay on a bed at one side of the hut, staring, without seeing, at a windeye just above his head, which at least afforded him fresh air. There was a barrel of water next to the bed. Smoke rose from a small fire in the middle of the floor. An old woman, spinning thread, stirred in the shadows as I stepped inside.

As I moved towards the bed, Cedd moved restlessly and began pressing his face into the pile of dirty rags under his head. Instantly the old woman dropped her thread and came forward to wipe his brow. I pulled out the salve. 'I've brought this for Cedd,' I said. 'It's made with honey.' The old woman did not look at me, but went on with her task. I repeated my offer, then, placing the salve on the floor, I said, 'Could I examine the wound? Perhaps I can help—I'm used to such injuries. Let me look.'

In the light of the windeye, the old woman seemed but a frail sack of old bones, that the wind might catch up and blow away, but when she laid her hand over mine, her steady grip was of iron. 'Look then!' she said and she took Cedd's face between her fingers and turned him into the light. The wound was an angry red line on his left cheek; his face burned bright with fever.

Cedd pushed his face into his pillow. There was a slick of damp on his skin, gleaming, as if the water of his life seeped out of him, drop by drop. He made no sound, as the old woman loosened her grip. She sat back in her dark corner. 'Oma,' I murmured—*grandmother*—and the crone twisted to look at me. 'The wound is too deep for the salve to work.' The oma cupped her hand into the barrel, held it over Cedd's lips and dripped cold water into his mouth. I bent forward to dip a rag to place on Cedd's forehead, but, with her hard old fingers, the old woman wrested the cloth from me, then went on with the task herself.

Close to, I studied the wound. It was a single cut from the edge of Grymma's dart, that had sliced across Cedd's face on its flight. Now I saw the grey matter gathering at the edges of the cut. It had already begun to fester.

'Fire,' I said, trying to think what Asa would do. 'It must be sealed.' I took out my blade and turned it hilt first to the old woman. She made no move to take it. 'Oma, the wound festers. It needs to be sealed with fire. If you won't do this, I must. Do you have ale? Cedd will need it to ease the pain.' As she got up to fetch ale from a goatskin, I turned to the fire to heat my blade.

The oma gave Cedd the ale, lifting his head to drink, then laying him carefully down as I prepared to seal the wound.

The blade soon grew red hot—hot enough—and I acted quickly, touching it lightly but firmly to the wound. Cedd gasped, once, and gritted his teeth against the pain. Then he lost his senses. It was Othinn's blessing. When he woke, the wound would be scoured of the poison, the pain would be less and his life saved.

'When Cedd wakes, use the salve,' I said. 'Just a smear on the wound.' The crone took the gift, dug her finger into the contents and tasted it. 'I'm on my way to the monastery,' I said. 'I'll send help.'

CHAPTER 13
THE SAXON MONASTERY

The sun was high as I rode up the track to the monastery, on its promontory looking over the sea. Before it was a stretch of open ground, close cropped by a dozen sheep, a goat, and a donkey.

The buildings of the monastery itself were enclosed by a fence of strong stakes, bound tightly together, in the middle of which was a pair of stout wooden gates. Above it, I saw the top of a square stone building like a grey block against the sky. Atop that was a tower, with a bell. All was still. Only the buzz of flies disturbed the silence.

As I came to the gates, they swung open. My approach had been noted: I had been deemed worthy of welcome. A monk, clothed and hooded in black, gestured to me to ride on to the central stone building, between a handful of thatch-roofed shelters, huddled under its protection like chicks round a mother hen.

According to the stories told in the Mark, the Saxon monasteries had pavements of marble and doors encrusted with gold. This did not look like a treasure house.

The track ended in an open place, where I dismounted, tying Snorri up to an ash post, set there for the purpose, it seemed. There was no one about. I had expected some kind of challenge; not a speeding dart, not that, but at least a word or two, demanding to know my purpose.

In the wall of the stone building ahead, a candle-flame, set in the windeye, flared into life, then, when I hammered on the door, a monk, silent, opened it.

'Berengeria Queen—' I called in a loud voice, and a pair of ravens flew noisily out of the belltower, with dry croaks and a flik-flak of their wings, '—here to see Father Anselm.'

The monk ushered me into a stone cell, a small place with three doors: one on my right hand, surely leading into the place beneath the belltower, one on my left, and one ahead, covered by a grey linen cloth which the monk pushed aside to allow me entrance. I stepped into another small place, lit by a candle. There was no windeye. But there was a bench and I sat to wait for Father Anselm to summon me.

I waited there for as long as I deemed fit, then thinking the monk had forgotten me, I pushed the grey cloth aside and stepped back into the place with three doors. A noise drew my attention to the door on the left. Perhaps the monk was inside. I pushed the handle, opened it and stepped into the place under the belltower.

This room was a large empty space, the length and width of one of our traders, *Ravenseye* or *Waverider*. It had an earth floor and logs for benches. There was no sign of the monk.

Long flickering shadows from candlelight led my eye up to the high roof, where the rafters showed like the bones of a ship, upside down. It was well made. With admiration I traced the pattern from the front to the back of the place. There my eye stopped, my blood chilled, as an image leapt to my sight from the shadows. I gasped and pressed myself back to the wall.

Othinn. It was Othinn, a wooden effigy of the god, as I had imagined it to be, from the tales I knew from my earliest childhood. He hung there, pinned to Yggdrasil, the great ash tree at the centre of the world. Here the tree was a cross, a huge cross, made of two long timbers. From the tree, Othinn looked down at me, his arms outstretched, his gaunt face lined and sad. Nine days and nine nights he hung there, unclothed, powerless to help himself, suffering like a thief or a beggar, to gain a great prize: the knowledge of the runes, of how to make marks that other men could read, and so pass on knowledge and understanding, by which means to gain great power.

Othinn. I pressed my hand to my mouth, hardly daring to take breath. Where was his eagle? Where was the snake that twined round Yggdrasil? Where was the bubbling spring of Mimir at its foot? Strange omissions.

Othinn. I knelt and bowed my head to him, trying to pray, but my words came out in a mangled cry, which I stifled at once. I curled my fists and stood up. Better to approach great Othinn head high and standing.

As I looked up at him, the door opened behind me. It was the silent monk, now gesturing me to follow.

I was led to another shelter, a little way behind the stone house, one room, ten strides or so long and wide, with a single doorway, across which fluttered a black cloth. Several candles gave light and their smoke had already gathered in the dim recesses of the roof space. There was a table and bench, bunches of herbs hanging from the rafters, a pile of straw in one corner, and nothing more.

There stood the man I came to know as Father Anselm. He was dressed like the others in a black woollen robe, his hair shorn, cut above the ears, his pate shaved. In his simple guise, this man was a leader. It showed in the tilt of his shaven chin and in the piercing stare of his sharp blue eyes.

'*Waes thu hael*,' he greeted me in Saxon. I returned the greeting. 'Please.' He gestured to the bench. 'Sit. Eat. Drink. Brother Guthric—'

The doorkeeper produced a brown jug and beakers and filled them. I sipped the drink. It was a smooth honey mead, very palatable, similar to that on which Asa prided herself.

Father Anselm took no refreshment for himself, but turned to the table and began to chop herbs, releasing the strong scent of woundwort. 'I've been expecting you,' he said, now using my own Viking tongue. 'How are things in the wood? One of your warriors has left the camp. Why was that?'

I choked on my drink and he swung round, laughing as I recovered. 'You see. Albinus has told me all about you.' He passed me a cloth.

'How do you come to speak my language?' I said, wiping my chin.

'Like you I'm a traveller. I have spent a deal of time in your land and elsewhere.' He gestured to the herbs on the bench, to the bunches drying overhead, and to a row of bottles and jars, set in a neat row on shelves in the dimmest corner. 'I'm a student of healing. I seek knowledge wherever it may be found and I am bound by my oath to use it to heal the sick of whatever race or creed. I thank God for it. Saxon, Viking, Celt, Arab. We are all brothers under the skin. We all bleed, we all suffer. I'm making a poultice for Cedd's wound.' His eyes searched mine as I related to him what I had done to heal the injury.

'A drastic remedy, but perhaps for the best. He's in God's hands then. I shall pray for him. Cedd's heart is sound, he's a leader, one we can't afford to lose.' He refilled my cup. 'You did well. Now tell me about the one who rode south.'

It was what I had come for, to explain my difficulty with my uncle and to try to persuade him that it would be helpful to both sides to form an alliance. Without interruption, going on with his task, Father Anselm listened to my tale.

When it was finished, he said:

'If, as you fear, Vasser Wulf and this Grymma return here with a Viking war band to claim this territory for themselves—if he believes, as this Grymma believes, that the only good Saxon is a dead Saxon—where will you stand? Will you stand with us? Or with your kin?'

His hand, gently cropping the herbs, was steady, but I knew he waited intently for my answer. I took my own time before giving it. I stood at a fork in the road; my next words would decide the tribe's future: there would be no going back.

'I crossed the river to mend things with Cedd, surely, but also to seek an alliance. My father-brother Vasser Wulf may challenge me for my crown when he returns—'

Father Anselm laughed out loud and scraped cut herbs into a bowl. 'Why should we help you to keep a crown? Do you then intend to rule over us? If we decide to join our strength to yours, it will be to keep this territory safe from all raiding predators, Viking or Saxon. Let me speak plainly. Our future certainly lies in an alliance. We shall live side by side here, as equals, bowing to no man, only to God, keeping the peace together.'

'I do not seek to rule over you,' I said, my voice shaking. 'I will lead my people—I am their queen—though perhaps it is time to give up that title. Whatever action I take will be for the good of us all, of whatever blood or belief, for my people in alliance with yours. We are sick of battle. We are here to settle and trade. We don't wish to fight. Soon Lord Guthrum will end the war—'

'Don't be so sure of that,' murmured Father Anselm. He shook his knife at me. 'Aelfred King will have something to tell about that.' I fell silent, my spirit unsure. Father Anselm left his task, came to me and put his hand on my shoulder.

'Whoever prevails in the southern war, I know that you sincerely seek peace, Berengeria Queen.' With a kind smile, he looked down at me. 'That much is clear from your actions—you have come here alone, risking your life. So, you are welcome. And you are right. We must stand together, whether to share food and medicines, or to defeat a common enemy. The way to peace is a hard road, but—' he took my hand and arm, in a firm grip, sealing a promise, 'we shall set foot on that road together.'

As a bell clanged dolefully over the monastery, Father Anselm's movements became brisk and businesslike. 'I must visit Cedd. I'll leave at once.' At the doorway, he turned back. 'We must hold moot, your people and mine, here at the monastery, tomorrow. Come, break bread with us.'

'We will come to the moot,' I said, formally accepting Father Anselm's invitation.

'Stay for a while now,' he said, as I followed him out of the hut. 'Ease your mind, Berengeria, you and your people will be quite safe as our guests. There will be no ambush, I assure you, we have nothing to hide.' He settled his pack over his shoulder. 'Look about you. Examine our treasures.'

Treasures? 'I will,' I said, glad of the chance to see them. Mounting his horse, Father Anselm signalled to one of the monks. 'Find Albinus,' he said. 'Tell him he has a visitor.'

CHAPTER 14
GREAT OTHINN'S CROSS

I pushed aside the door cloth and walked back to the central place, in front of the stone building, from where I could see more of the layout of the whole monastery. Inside its enclosure, the settlement was much bigger than I had thought. There were at least twenty small huts and three larger shelters, used, as I guessed, for care of the sick or for moot. Smoke rose from one and I could smell roasting meat: that must be where the monks broke fast together.

No one challenged me. With their arms full of baskets or carrying tools, wood, and cloth, the monks hurried about their business, but, when I stepped out to stand in a patch of sunshine, one of them, his arms tucked into wide sleeves, blocked my path.

'Waes hael,' I said. He did not return my greeting. 'I'm waiting for Albinus.'

The monk inclined his head. 'Brother Albinus is in discipline,' he said, gesturing that I should wait inside the hut, so I stepped back into the cold murk, tucked up the door cloth and sat on the bench with my thoughts.

What a strange treasure house the monastery was. So far I had seen no sign of anything that might tempt raiders. Our tales told of mountains of gold, rivers of silver and jewels, kept in the Saxon monasteries. Rich silk cloths, finely damascened swords. Where was it all? Why would you keep it hidden? Why would anyone keep chests full of great riches and not use them to prove their standing, win friends, and provide a comfortable existence? If I had treasure I would use it to buy a fine chair and table, an oak bed with a feather pillow and a house for Raed. She would have the best perch and the finest hood and I would place silver ties on her talons, with bells that would ring if she flew out of sight.

I longed to see the sky, so I stood up again and went to the door. Albi was crossing the yard. 'Halloo! Well met!'

As I smiled in response, the mournful clang of a bell rang—once, twice, thrice. The other monks quickly put down their bundles and turned towards the stone building where the great image of Othinn hung.

'What's happening?' I said.

'Prayers. I'm excused going, since I'm unworthy at the moment. I'm supposed to pray by myself. I was meant to spend the whole day by myself—*incommunicado*—to reflect on my weaknesses. Father Anselm has excused me, because you're here.' We exchanged a grin. The bell clanged again and, when the monks were all gathered inside, there followed the deep rumble of men's voices, chanting words or singing to no tune I could follow, all on two or three notes.

Albi ducked into the hut and threw himself down on the bench. He sat forward resting his hands on his knees, draped with the lap of his robe.

'Father Anselm said I could look round. Will you show me the monastery?' I began.

'I'd be glad to,' he said, moving up to make room for me on the bench. 'Once Terce is over and the others have left the church.'

'Tair-ss?'

'Prayers.'

'Cherrich?'

He shoved me towards the doorway and pointed to the stone building. 'The church.'

As we sat down again, I thought what a strange life it was, this life of prayers and discipline.

Albi tapped his knees. 'It's good to see you,' he said. 'What brings you here?'

I told him what had happened to Cedd. 'Father Anselm has gone to see him? He was in such a temper this morning, pacing the herbarium, adding a curse to every stride. "*God's blood and bones*," he said.' Albi sat up and chuckled. ' "*By Our Lady!*" he said. "*Hell!*" He wanted hellebore, but Cerdic had used the last without telling him and he had none ready.'

'Asa has hellebore,' I said. 'I'll bring some for him.'

'Anselm has spoken to us about you. That's why you were allowed inside the monastery. He thinks we can help each other. He says it will be best for all of us to at least try to live in peace. He's asked the brothers to trust you.' At this I smiled and Albi said, 'It will take more than healing a single wound.'

'It's a start.'

'Yes.'

For some breaths we sat silent. I was pleased by Albi's speech; it seemed another step towards peace. Then I saw his fingers gather the cloth of his robe on his knees and bunch it into his fists. Staring at the ground, he blurted his words: 'If the raiders come back here, whose side will you choose?'

I had my answer ready.

'We want peace as much as anyone.'

'But what will you do? Will you fight your own kin?'

I leaned forward and said my say as leader of my tribe once more, to calm Albi's fears. Perhaps I would have to keep saying it, until the Saxons, all of them, believed me.

'I am no raider, and I shall not stand aside to watch innocent people killed. I came here to seek allies. If we look to share food and skills, we must share the land and defend it together.'

Albi nodded. We sat silent. Then I said: 'Do you remember when we were in that large cavern in the Hill and I saw the fox?'

'Yes, and I didn't.'

'Do you believe the gods speak to us in dreams?'

'I believe *God* does that sometimes.'

'Well, I dreamt I was inside the cavern and saw the fox again.'

'The mysterious fox,' Albi said, as if he did not believe me.

'I *did* see it.'

'All right. Go on.'

'It climbed the wall and disappeared through the roof. Is there a gap there? Big enough for a fox to climb through?'

Albi shook his head. 'I've never seen one.' His face lit with excitement. 'We could take a look if you like. Just to put your mind at rest.'

'Tonight?'

He nodded. 'At dusk. I'll get myself put *incommunicado* again so that I miss evensong.'

For a long breath I watched Albi's eyes on fire with the thought of a new adventure. He saw no danger, but I was beginning to feel it creeping towards us like sea mist on a distant horizon. 'Bring a weapon,' I said.

Albi picked the iron cross from his chest. 'This is all the weapon I need against demons,' he said.

The sound of monks' voices plumed into the yard. 'Amen. Amen. Amen.' The monks were filing out of the stone building.

Albi and I left the hut. 'I should say at least one prayer.'

'Do it then,' I said.

'All right.' Albi dropped to his knees, bowed his head, clasped his hands and began to mutter into his robe. Then he stopped. 'Why don't you pray too?' he said, encouraging me with a nod.

'All right, but we don't pray on our knees.' I threw back my head and my arms wide. 'GR-EAT OTH-INNN!' I began.

Albi tugged at my shirt.

'You couldn't pray to Jesus, could you?'

'Gheez? Who is this Gheez? Why should I pray to him? My god is Othinn. And yours too, by the look of things. You have Othinn's image in your cherrach.'

'Ch-urr-ch.'

'Cherr-urr-ch.'

'There's no image of Othinn there.'

'Yes there is. I've seen it.' I moved towards the church door, which was still open. The few remaining monks were going about their tasks again.

'Show me this Othinn,' Albi said, following me inside.

We stared up at the great wooden cross as I told Albi about great Othinn, and of how he was pinned by a spear to the world tree Yggdrasil, for nine days and nine nights. Then he told me the story of great Gheez, who was put on a tree and died there, scorned and shamed, because he, a god, walked the earth as a man.

'What are runes?' Albi said.

'Signs. *Writing*. Do you have clay and a stick? I'll show you.'

'I can do better than clay and a stick,' Albi said. 'Follow me.'

CHAPTER 15
THE WRITING

The hut we entered, a scribe's hut, as Albi called it, for this *writing*, which seemed to be the scribe monk's sole daily task, was larger than the first and contained a table, a chair, and another image of great Gheez, hanging on his cross, the god who turned himself into a man and got killed to shame us all. His story haunted my head. It made no sense. Why didn't he save himself? My mind played on this as if it were a sore tooth. Why would a god make himself so weak? Yet Othinn had done a similar thing to learn the runes. I must talk to Asa about it.

The table stood beneath a wide windeye, which afforded it clear light. Albi pulled out a chest from under the table, took off the lid and began to remove the contents, piece by piece, handling them as if they were treasures.

There was a small wooden frame, a hand's breadth, on which was stretched a piece of hide so thin that I could see the shadow of my fingers through it. Next, Albi unplugged a small jar and showed me the black liquid inside.

'Ink,' he said. He sniffed the jar, screwed up his nose then offered it to me.

'Phaugh. It stinks,' I said.

Albi laughed. 'Ink stink,' he said.

Next he took out a long goose feather and held it up to the light. 'Hold out your strongest hand,' he said. I held out my right hand. Albi twisted the feather in his fingers, then put it back and took out a different one.

'What's wrong with this one?' I said, picking up the first feather.

'The curve of the shaft is wrong. See? It curves, one way or the other, depending on which wing it comes from, left or right. You need one from the right wing to fit your grasp.'

He held up the new feather then drew a knife and cut off the vanes either side of the shaft. Then he cut straight across the end and finally made a small cut up the shaft. 'Penna,' he said.

I still had no idea what he was talking about.

'These runes,' he said. 'Show me.'

It took me several attempts to make a mark on the hide with the penna, but finally I had scratched two signs: *aesc* for Albinus and *beorc* for Beren.

'A and B!' Albi took the penna and scratched his own runes. As I watched the signs taking shape I prayed: *Great Othinn forgive me.* I knew what Asa would say, that it was forbidden to write the runes, that they had great power for good and ill.

Albi held out the penna and said: 'Show me the rest.'

My hand faltered. 'You write something now,' I said, pushing the penna away.

While Albi wrote, I looked at other pieces of *writing*

that lay in the chest. One piece had on it a picture of warriors, wearing helmets and wielding war axes above their heads. There were many black ink marks on the hide. *Writing*. Perhaps it was a story, a skald's tale that I could later tell to Asa.

I asked Albi to tell me what it said.

'No,' he said and clumsily shoved the piece back into the chest. We locked stares.

'Tell me!' I said. 'Read the *writing*!'

Albi's mouth set in a stubborn line. I pulled the piece from the chest.

'It's about the raid, isn't it? These warriors—they're Vikings, aren't they? You'd better read it. Read it for me. I want to know.'

Albi took the writing from me. 'Very well. Sit there,' he said. 'Don't move. Don't speak. And when I've finished, remember that you asked me to do this.'

I sat on the stool and nodded.

Albi began to read.

'*None looked out to sea when the ravens came.*
When they knocked at the door—weary travellers—
Father Abbot let them in: guests carrying their bloodgift.
Iron fist. Stone heart. Steel blade.
Men died on earth. Ravens blackened the sky.
Blood made the grey stones red.
They burned the books. They danced on the embers.
Thieves stole the gold hoard
Cross, cup, and platen.
The dead watched them.'

Memory washed the tale clear for me, like ice water on pebbles. How many times had I heard raiding tales sung by the skald at my father's hearth, but his skald sang of raids on enemy strongholds, not on monasteries like this. He sang tales of battle, the ding of swords, of keen eye and strong arm. A pang like a plucked string flexed in my chest. Vikings had slaughtered unarmed scribes and monks here, in an unprovoked attack.

I put out my hand to touch the table and saw, in my mind's eye, the scribe, unaware of approaching death, wrapped in his black habit, shoulders hunched against the icy saltwind that blew through the windeye. All silence, except for the soft scrape of the goosefeather quills on the vellum, now and again a closed cough or a gasp as he came to the end of a line of black signs, or a low groan as he stretched his back and neck, before bending again to the task.

A bell rang like an alarm to my thoughts. Albi stopped reading and hastily bundled the vellum back into the chest, as Father Anselm entered the hut. 'Albinus, your meal is ready in the refectory. Go now.' Albi bowed his head then left.

I followed Father Anselm outside and took some deep breaths of fresh air to clear my head as we walked together back towards the outer gate. 'Cedd's wound will heal,' he said. 'That honey salve is a most useful remedy. Ask your stepmother Asa if she would trade for the receipt.' Unable to speak I nodded, but when I untied Snorri's reins, Anselm stood in front of me and put his hands on my shoulders.

'What is it? Are you in pain?'

I shook my head. 'Albinus told me about the raid—'

'There are evil men everywhere, not just in your community. I hope we can learn to judge one another by our deeds not by what tribe we belong to.'

'But if the raiders came back—'

'We will defend ourselves.'

As if to prove his words a group of monks armed with staves appeared behind him. Anselm turned to face them, a look of surprise on his face.

'Move aside, Father,' said one, with stern purpose. 'Give us the Viking. She will learn what it is to despoil a holy place and pay for such disrespect with her blood.' One of the monks held a rope. Another a faggot of birch twigs. Was I in for a beating?

'Despoil a holy place?' Anselm swung round to me. 'What does he mean?'

Before I could answer Albi pushed his way through the crowd. 'I took her into the church.' There were gasps and cries of outrage.

'She stood in the sanctuary!', 'Under the Rood!', 'Her head bare!'

'Peace, brothers!' Anselm called. 'Albinus, is this true?'

'Yes, Father. She wanted to see the Great Cross for herself.'

'She may become a Christian?' asked one of the monks.

I stepped forward and pulled Asa's silver cross from my pack.

'This is for Father Abbot,' I said, speaking in Saxon. 'There is no charge. It is a gift.' I stepped back and bowed my head, to avoid meeting their angry eyes. So Asa taught me to behave when faced by a snarling wolf. It worked. The monks lowered their weapons.

'This is a generous gift,' said Anselm. 'Brother Titus, it seems the fault yet again belongs to our young friend, Albinus, albeit a minor fault. It may be that this Viking girl will be brought, in time, to the faith through Albinus's actions. God moves in most mysterious ways.'

The monks muttered their agreement.

'Nonetheless there was a fault—Albinus should have sought permission for his action—so, what punishment would you have for him?'

Brother Titus threw out his chest like a puffing pigeon. 'Albinus should remain in solitary contemplation for the rest of the week. With only one meal a day. No breakfast nor supper. He must pray for the forgiveness of his brothers and ask for it publicly at noon tomorrow.'

'Very well.' Father Anselm nodded his agreement.

Solitary. Alone again. It was what Albi had hoped for. As he was led away he managed to sneak a glance back at me. There was a smile on his lips.

CHAPTER 16
'GOD CURSE THAT NAME...'

Asa was away with Helga and the others, washing clothes in the river, when I returned to the camp, so, snatching bread with a smear of curd cheese, I went straight to the hawk pens.

It was a comfort to see Raed almost well again, to feel her weight on my arm as her claws dug deeply into my wristguard, and to see her bright eye, still and shining like a peat pool on the moors. Whatever else changed in my life, she did not change.

Skar was tending the other hawks, choosing which to fly, which to rest, moving calmly among his charges, stroking feathers or offering shreds of meat, as if he were back in the Mark, and there had been no battle, no voyage, no new camp to build, and no concerns about Vasser Wulf. Alone with Skar and Raed, my mind settled.

Raed was anxious to fly again. She was watchful, alert, her bright eye missing nothing. Her head moved in slight, tiny jinks to north and south or in smooth turns, as if well-greased, to east, to west, her beak, with its curved deadly point, lifted, smelling the air to scent danger. Stabbing was her game. I looked at her with fresh eyes, asking myself why the gods make such creatures. Such killers.

Then I remembered Thorkil's teaching, that all wild things live in balance: hawks feed on sparrows, sparrows on worms. Worms feed on plants. Plants on earth. Earth on stones. The balance must be kept if the world is to stay in good health.

What about Man? I had asked him.

'Man has free will,' he replied. 'He is master of all and may choose, to kill or not, and face the consequences.'

Had Vasser made a free choice? To kill my father or to have him killed? Why?

Skar pushed a lump of raw meat into my hand, which I offered to Raed. She stabbed it greedily then tossed her head and swallowed it in one gulp.

Skar held up four fingers and pointed to the sky.

Winternight. Less than a month away. 'I know! I know!' I said, irked to be reminded. One month to Vasser's return. Skar stroked Raed and adjusted her tether.

'Tomorrow at first light, then,' I said. 'We'll follow the river to the south and see what game's there.'

The day was losing its heat when I set out for the Hill. As I approached, it glowed in the setting sun, seeming harmless.

Would I see the fox again? *If there is a message, Othinn, grant me clear understanding,* I breathed, as, leaving the wood, a flight of homing rooks fluttered noisily over my head.

Leaving Snorri at the foot of the Hill, I began to climb and came to the cave entrance unchallenged. Catching breath, I looked back at her, now a small toy horse far below. A hand clapped itself to my shoulder.

'There you are!'

In a move without thought, I ducked and swung, crouching with fists clenched, ready to trade blows. Gasping, Albi fell back, then, muttering something, slipped off his shoes and flexed his toes, digging his right forefinger between them. I picked up one of his shoes and tipped the gravelly sand from it.

'Discipline again?'

'Mm,' he said, attending to his toes. '*You* are in my debt. I hate sand. It was Titus's punishment for what *you* did with your praying—*Great Othinn . . .* ' Albi's imitation of my prayer made me laugh, but I gave him a shove for his cheek.

Albi sat with his back to the cave and bent over his feet. 'Agh—ugh—ooh—' he growled, until I could stand no more. I pulled out my water sack and splashed his feet with cold water.

'Enough! Enough!' he cried, shaking his feet in the air. 'They're clean! They're clean now! Thank you!' I stopped and he snatched up his shoes and put them on. 'Not really suited to the monastic life, am I?'

'What life would you choose, if you had the choice?' I re-stoppered the sack, then sat at his side, looking back down the Hill.

'I want to travel to the edge of the world. I want to see great cities. I want to—oh—explore and find out all there is to know.' There was a pause, then he said: 'Once things are settled in the south.'

I looked down at Snorri. 'That conflict is almost over. Lord Guthrum will force Aelfred King to make terms. Why wait? Could you not leave now?'

'I'm needed here, we all are. We have to keep ourselves battle-ready, in case of another attack—' shamefaced, Albi shrugged, 'I owe it to Father Anselm.' He would not meet my eyes.

'Were you here during the raid?'

'No. I was visiting our father-house in the west. I came back at the start of the summer.'

'Just as well that you missed it—you're no warrior.'

'No, I'm not, not by choice. But I will carry a sword if I have to.' Albi gave me a determined stare. 'I won't stand by and let raiders attack the monastery again.'

'Nor will I,' I said quickly, keeping my eyes on his. Albi smiled and I nodded to confirm what I'd said. So there it was. The word spoken, the promise made.

'Do you think it's possible for Vikings and Saxons to live together?' I said. 'So far, we have traded little.'

'Because the villagers have nothing to trade with.' Albi sighed and rubbed his face. 'Cedd's task, as soon as he wakes from his bed every day, is to find enough kindling to make the hearth fires. Next he has to grub up enough meal to make bread. Without help from St Bede's they would starve. And worse—when they scavenge for grain in the fields, what they find is burnt bones. Every day Cedd gives out tasks and chores to keep their hands busy and their minds free of dark memories—'

'What can I do? Where do I start?'

'Start by sharing your food. Don't try to barter. Give it freely. Keep nothing back. Let Father Anselm be the arbiter. Let him divide the stores according to need.'

'My people will never agree to it. We don't have enough. Just today my fowler reminded me that we need more meat set aside for Winternight.'

'Winternight? What's that?'

'It's our long-held tradition—a celebration for harvest, a thanksgiving for safe harbour, before the onset of winter. We play games and tell stories and riddles, and, to honour Great Othinn, we hold a feast.'

Albi jumped to his feet.

'A *feast*? You're going to celebrate and have a *feast*, in full view of Cedd and the others? Beren, they're *starving*.'

'No—I—' I faltered, hauling myself up.

'You may have to change your traditions to settle here,' Albi said. I stared at the sunset. The Saxon village at the edge of the wood glowed red as if it were on fire.

'Vasser Wulf,' I murmured. 'He's coming back. He's on his way. He'll be here by Winternight.'

'Who?'

'Vasser Wulf. A great warrior. My father-brother. My uncle.' For the time being, I kept the rest of it to myself.

Albi too fell into a deep and long silence. Then he repeated the name. 'Vasser Wulf?'

'You know him?' I said.

Albi sighed and came to stand next to me. 'You were bound to find out one way or another. The name— Vasser Wulf—is mentioned in the account of the raid. I didn't finish reading it, did I? I had to stop when the bell rang for the midday meal and Father Anselm came to find me.'

'Tell me what it says. Can you remember?'

'I think so.' Albi cleared his throat then began to recite the words:

> *'Thieves stole the gold hoard.*
> *Cross, cup, and platen.*
> *The dead watched them do it.*
> *The dead watched and could not stir*
> *Rise up wrathful against robbers.*
> *Vasser Wulf was the worst.*
> *God curse that name.'*

As if from a great distance, I heard Albi say: 'There's more, I think—a long list of torments that await this Wulf in the several regions of Hell.' He kept his voice light as if he were telling me old news about strangers, but I heard his words as if they were nails driven into my flesh.

'*Great Othinn—*' I breathed, but I was not able to go on with the prayer. Perhaps Othinn heard what I was trying to say, and finally granted me clear understanding, because, like pieces of a puzzle falling into place, all the things I knew and remembered now showed in their final pattern.

Vasser had been here before. '*A pleasant land, good for farming. We'll make a new life there. There will be no resistance. No major Saxon settlement within a week's hard riding. Too far north for Aelfred and his thanes to bother with, but you must set seawatch for Harald of Norway.'* My uncle's words had issued from his mouth as easily as fat dripping from the meat he chewed. *'Trade with passing travellers on a great road that runs due north. Set watch there for northern raiders. You'll have plenty of time to fix boundaries and defences. Set them as widely as you can comfortably manage.'* He had made it sound so easy and reasonable but there were gaps in the truth of his words wide enough to drive a dragonship through. Our new life was to be built on the ravaged remains of a Saxon village, on the burnt bones of Cedd's family and the others. Our Saxon neighbours and the inhabitants of the monastery had not been part of his plan: and it was his plan, I saw it now. What I had taken for my uncle's advice was merely a set of orders to someone who would take a lesser place when he returned.

I realized Albi was speaking.

'This Vasser Wulf may not be the same person.'

'The same,' I said, hugging myself against this terrible knowledge. 'He is the same. He is the one, the one who led the raid here last spring. He is my father's brother.' I swung round to face Albi. 'When my father Thorkil died in battle for the Mark, Vasser led us here to safety in exile. He knew this place and told us about it. He said the few Saxons who still lived here would welcome us as traders and settlers, that they were people who remembered where their ancestors had come from, that they recognized us as kin and would share the land, good for farming. He said nothing of any raid.'

I covered my face.

Albi put his hands over mine and pulled them away, so that I had to look into his eyes.

'He will not seek peace with Saxons, will he?'

I shook my head.

'When will he be here?'

'I don't know—within a month—'

For several breaths we stood, separate and apart, with nothing to say to each other.

'The light's going,' Albi said suddenly. 'If you want to explore the Hill we'd better go in there now.'

'Let's go to the cavern,' I said bleakly. For the time being we were back on safe ground. I turned and ducked into the cave entrance.

CHAPTER 17
THE CAVERN

O nce, Thorkil had shown me a curious thing, a bauble traded from an Arabian scholar, a solid object with six square sides, a Roman *cubus,* perhaps, a gaming die, made of cedarwood, richly painted in glowing colours, each side marked with a different letter in the language of Rome called Latin.

He had watched me examine every detail of the pattern on each side, as he had taught—*'let nothing pass'*—but I kept coming back to the side where the letter B was painted in green and gold, my favourite colours. 'That's my favourite,' I said.

With a twist of his fingers Thorkil had unfolded the die and laid it flat so that it made the shape of a cross and showed its whole meaning. Six letters spelled out a word: *BEATUS* meaning 'blessed'. Was it the name of the owner, or a wish for good luck in the game?

'A king or queen,' Thorkil said, 'must not have favourites. He or she must see every side, then consider the whole.' *See every side* . . . There were more sides yet to the pattern—I could not yet see the whole—but I was beginning to.

Another memory came to me. I won a fight once, in the Mark, against a boy who had thought to win wordfame by besting Thorkil's daughter. As he entered the ring, I saw Vasser viciously stab the top of the boy's arm with the point of his blade.

The boy, not willing to show pain in front of his friends, came to the fight with gritted teeth and curled fists. But I did not like what I had seen. I would not fight an opponent so deliberately weakened.

I couldn't draw scorn on my family by revealing my uncle's behaviour, so I changed the terms of contest. Instead of a wrestling bout I would lock forearms with the boy across a bench, making sure the boy would use his strong arm.

The boy still lost the contest: Vasser had taken away his heart. My opponent learned that he would not be permitted to best me: the injustice weakened his spirit. Just as the raids, vicious, unjust attacks against ill-prepared opponents, weakened the spirit of the Saxons. It was a vile way to win a war. It would never be my way.

I pulled at Albinus's sleeve.

'Whatever is decided by moot, I and my people shall fight Vasser Wulf and his men alone,' I said. 'There is a blood debt to pay.'

I followed him into the cavern and helped to place torches around the echoing space until every dark corner was illumined, as if for a special moot in some vast underground hall.

'You can't do it alone,' Albi said and a scornful laugh escaped me before I could stop it.

'What help can you or Father Anselm offer?' The cave

rang with my shouts. 'When Vasser Wulf comes he will bring his warrior band with him. Fighting men. His trained wolves. If they turn on the monastery, no one will survive. They are all of them killers! *Ber-serker*.' The word left my mouth as if it were something sour to be spat out. I looked at Albi, and was sorry for the look of shock on his face.

'When the fit is on them,' I said, more calmly, 'they are nothing more than wild beasts and they relish battle. They tear bodies like carcasses and drink their enemy's blood!'

Albi nodded. 'You fear them.'

'No!'

'Yes, you do. That's why you're shouting and making things up! I don't believe they drink blood!'

I laughed without joy.

'What happens when the fit is gone? What then? Do they become farmers and makers again? Fathers and husbands? Of course they do. The women warriors too. We are all human. Under the skin we are all the same.'

I made for the tunnel. Albi barred my path. 'We *are* all the same. Saxons, Vikings, Celts—we could all be *ber-serker*, if we were pushed far enough. Beren, listen to me—' Albi spoke urgently into my face. 'The monks spend their lives trying to tame the wildness. *Ber-serk*. Why do you think they all wear Benedict's cloth and obey the call of the bells?' I shrugged, and when he stepped aside, I turned back into the cavern. 'No one is born *ber-serk*. Killers are made so. I wonder what pushed Vasser Wulf to such a pitch?'

'Warriors must fight to the death,' I said. 'Blood deeds bring honour.' I spoke the words I had been taught to say, an empty repetition.

'We might not have to fight. Have you ever killed anyone?' Albi said.

'Have you?'

'No. I practise my fighting skills with wooden swords and blunt arrows, but I can wrestle!' I gave an honest laugh at that—Albi was as slight as a sparrow. Then we laughed together and the fearspell that held me broke apart.

'I'm not sure I could kill someone,' Albi said.

'In battle, you would fight to the death. Even you. Mostly you kill without knowing it. Afterwards I pray that Othinn will guide all the dead, from both sides, to Valhal.'

'Do you know to the day when Vasser Wulf will come?'

I leaned into the cold hardness of the rock. 'He said he would be here for Winternight.' I stood up, shivering, as I saw the bare truth, creeping into the light. 'If he finds Saxons here, he'll wipe them out.'

Albi took my hand in a firm warm grip.

'He will not,' he said. 'If you mean what you've said, if you will stand against this man, your own kin, to stay here, you must bring your people over the river, to the monastery. That is what I shall say at the moot. There's no room for mistrust. Bring your food, bring your weapons, everything—hold nothing back—and we'll face Vasser Wulf together—Saxons and Vikings side by side.'

'What about Cedd?' I said.

'Cedd will not stand against you. He knows which is the milch cow.'

'But where are your warriors? Who will fight? You said the monks spend their lives taming themselves to a life of peace.'

'If it comes to it, we shall fight for our freedom as much as the next man.'

'We must make more weapons then,' I said, turning sharply towards the exit.

'Whoa, nag! Aren't you forgetting something?' Albi said. He waved a wedge of bread at me. 'Point One: it's dark. We can do nothing until first light. Point Two: I haven't finished my supper yet. Point Three: you haven't started yours.' He threw the bread at me: I stuck out my hand just in time. 'Point Four: cast your mind back to the monastery. I was made *incommunicado*, right?'

'I haven't time for this—'

'Which meant I could miss evensong and sneak out to join you? To look for your imaginary fox?'

Shock poured over me; how could I have forgotten my reason for being here? To discover the message brought by the fox, my father's soulspirit. *Great Othinn, forgive me. Thorkil, father, forgive me.* 'Why didn't you say?'

'I just did.'

I threw down the bread and began searching the wall for an opening, any gap that the fox could have slipped through. Albi scrambled to his feet, brushing crumbs off his habit. 'No fox in here. You'd smell it.'

'It was here. And it climbed to the top of the wall. Up these ledges look—here and here. Three steps and a jump to the top.' I held my torch high to look up at the spot where in my *'seeing'* the fox had vanished. 'There might be a way through.' I spotted a dark slash near the roof, which looked like a crevice. 'I need to get up there.'

'God help me,' said Albi, as he bent over and cupped his hands. 'Leg up then.'

I put my foot in his hands and, with a mighty heave for a sparrowbones, he lifted me until I was able to balance with one foot on a ledge and the other on his right shoulder.

'What can you see?' he said.

'Not a lot,' I said, hauling myself up the wall to stand with both feet on a wider ledge. I stood on tiptoe to reach as high up as I could but the crevice was still out of reach, by an arm's length. 'Hold up your torch,' Albi said suddenly, 'as high as it will go.'

'What's the good of that if I can't see?'

'Just do it.'

Stung, I thrust the torch above my head and pressed it as close as I could to the site of the crevice. My right cheek was jammed against the rock. 'What now?'

'See for yourself.'

Mumbling a curse I grazed my cheek slowly across the rock, until I could see the torch. Then I forgot the discomfort of the graze. The flames were fierce and lying flat at the top of the stump of reeds. 'There's a stiff breeze,' I said. 'There must be an opening.'

'See if you can get up there,' Albi said.

'No,' I said jumping down. 'We'll make a ladder.'

We fetched branches from Albi's den, gathered for kindling, and, using our knives, cut two long stakes for the sides and ten rungs, tying them together with strips cut from the bottom of Albi's cloak.

From the top of the ladder I could easily see the gap through which my fox had disappeared.

It was the size of a large handspan, big enough for a fox to get through, big enough to look through.

'What do you see?'

'Can't see anything,' I said.

'Pass me the torch,' he said. 'You'll see better without it. You'll get your night eyes if you wait.'

'I know that,' I said. I passed him the torch, then turned to look into the gap as far as I could. Getting night eyes takes time and I had to fight the fear that the ladder might give way or that all the torches would go out. Then I began to see.

CHAPTER 18
'THIS IS VASSER'S DOING...'

I could see the sea. On the other side of a dark space was a great jagged opening, then an expanse of blue moonlit strand, then the sea. The breeze beat on my face and I took deep breaths. Sea wind, salt smell. Breath of the gods taking me home.

'What do you see?' Albi repeated.

'There's another cave. Huge. Open to the sea. It's a choppy tide. There's lots of white on the breakers.'

'I wonder which bay it is? There are so many along the coast here. Any landmarks?'

'No.' I stared deep into the darkness of the cave itself, trying to make sense of its shadows. There was one shape in the middle, more solid than the rest. I traced a long curve, then stopped and pulled back from the gap.

'What is it?' Albi hissed.

A man had stepped into the entrance to the cave. In the light of his torch, when he threw back his cloak, I saw a long jagged tear in the cloth. It was the hooded stranger, the watcher in the wood. When he turned his face into the torchlight, my heart beat like a trapped bird. It was Einar. One of Vasser's most trusted henchmen.

'What—?' Albi said, still holding the ladder. I shook my head at him and passed my thumb swiftly across my mouth to tell him to be quiet as death. Then I looked through the gap again. Was Einar alone? It seemed so. He walked into the cave and his torchlight flickered over the dark shape in the centre, over the proud head of the dragon, over its jutting eyes, over the long curve of the gunwale, over the gold shield that lay at its heart. I shrank back as if struck by a blow.

'What is it? What do you see? Come down now. It's my turn.' Carefully I climbed down and set myself on solid ground. Albi started to climb, then stopped. 'Your face is ashen,' he said. 'Sit down. Have some water.'

Pressing back to the rock, I shook my head and began to speak, though my voice shook on the words.

'My father's ship. *Swanwing*. It's there in the cave.' I covered my face with my hands as angry tears wet my fingers. 'I don't understand! Why is my father's ship here? I watched it burn!' Albi handed me a rag to wipe my face. I cried again, loud angry tears, and banged the dull wall with my fists.

'Tell me exactly what you saw.'

'I saw my father's ship.'

'Are you certain?'

'I saw his gold shield, the one we laid on his body—' I shuddered. Albi pressed his hand hard on my shoulder. 'I saw Einar, Vasser's man. He's in the cave. He's been spying on us, from the beginning. Ever since we landed. Oh!' I shoved my head back to the rock. 'Vasser never trusted me. He's had me watched.' Briefly I told Albi about the watcher in the wood. 'Einar will have told Vasser everything. Why is my father's ship here?' I shouted. 'This is Vasser's doing. I know it is. Where is Thorkil's body?' My voice rose to shout again, but after that, I couldn't go on.

'We'll go to the cave,' Albi said. 'We need a boat.'

I looked up at him. 'My father sent the shadow soul to tell me.'

'Shadow soul?'

'The fox.'

Albi gave me a wry smile and began to pack his bag. 'Oh yes, the fox.'

I didn't try to persuade him to my view. What was the point? Albi had his faith and I had mine. I stood up. 'I must find a way to that cave.'

'I'll come with you, but we need a boat.'

I stood up and pressed my hands and face to the rock below the crevice. 'My father's death ship is on the other side of this rock. I have to see it for myself.'

Albi was already quenching the torches. 'We can get there but we need a *boat*,' he said. This time I was listening.

'I know where to find one,' I said.

CHAPTER 19
THE HOODED STRANGER

Astride Snorri, we raced down the Hill, thanking the bright moon that shed its clouds to light our path, and made for the river. We crossed noisily, but no one stopped us going into the settlement. With a gentle nudge of my heels I prompted Snorri between the huts and along the seaward path, pushing through thicket and thorn, until we came within reach of the shore. At the edge of the wood, I tied her to a sapling and Albi and I threw ourselves on top of a dune to look down at the tribe's two boats, where Tyr kept ward. All here was peaceful. We crept closer.

Ravenseye lay high and wide as a stranded whale, a domed black shadow on the pale grey sand. Nothing moved. Tyr must be lost in ale-sleep.

Then a shadow broke from the ship and moved to sit beside it. Moonlight glinted on the bright edge of a spear. Tyr. How could I have doubted him?

'Who's that?' Albi's voice sounded loud in my ear.

I tossed a stone to land next to where Tyr sat. On the instant he was up. 'Who's there?'

'Friends!' I replied, as Albi and I slithered down the bank to join him.

'You have news?'

'Nothing, but, until we know for certain what Vasser intends, we must expect the worst.'

'To fight?'

'Yes.'

Tyr put his hand firmly on mine. 'You can depend on me.'

'I know,' I said. 'When the time comes, I'll send for you. We need the faering,' I said, gesturing to Tyr's own small fishing boat, the *Sea Elf*, upturned on the strand.

'Take it. It's yours.' Tyr was looking at Albi.

'Albinus, monk apprentice from St Bede's, the monastery on the other side of the river,' Albi said, with a slight bow.

I was untying the faering. 'I vouch for him,' I said and Tyr nodded.

When the *Sea Elf* was launched and Albi and I were safely on board, I called to Tyr on the shore: 'If anyone asks, we've gone fishing.'

'Let me come with you!'

'No. I need you to stay here. Keep a close watch. If you don't see us by dawn, go to the settlement.'

As Tyr nodded and waved, Albi and I bent ourselves to the oars.

I set to rowing and soon felt better than I had in weeks, with the sea's salt breath in my face, the rise and fall of the swell, the slap and hiss of the waves on the boat's sides.

As we rounded the rocks into the next bay, which enclosed the river estuary, I thought of the last time I had seen it from seaward. That was when we first came here to this land, exiles from the Mark.

Memories of that voyage rose in my mind. Vasser had quickly driven far ahead in his dragonship as if on a raid. Following in *Ravenseye*, I had soon lost sight of him: we had to guide ourselves to landfall. The fear-worm gnawed in my belly. What was his plan? To kill us all?

We stopped rowing and drifted for a while on the outward tide, and I flexed my shoulders and rolled my head, remembering how my body had ached after hours of rowing, the sail useless against a wind that seemed bent on driving us back to the Mark. I had fought a different enemy that day, pressed by fear and grief and shame and white-hot anger that burned inside me like bitter bile. Brand had taken my oar, and pointed me to rest with the others in the hollow of the boat: Brokk and Arn, their warrior faces set like stone, Finn, with young Gerd tucked under his cloak, Leif grasping a coiled rope he had salvaged and Helga gripping a store barrel, Skar with his hawks' cages tied to the benches, knocking against Snorri's hindquarters and the goats. But I had shaken my head and gone to stand at the prow, my feet clinging to the edge of the rail, defying the gods to take me, my arm round the neck of the raven, whose sleek head with its deadly beak jutted out over the sea.

Stinging rain had lashed my face, high waves had

broken over the boat. I could have jumped and given my burden to the sea. But I didn't.

'Look!' Albi called me back to the present, pointing to something on the distant shore.

We had rowed up the coast, past several small bays, each round and jagged, as if a giant had taken bites out of the land, hidden coves that made it easy for an enemy to land in secret. Fearing to go too far, we had kept watch for the dome of the Hill, but it was dark and the sea was choppy, and we had difficulty keeping the *Sea Elf* steady enough to get our bearings, so that on our first pass we didn't see it. Now, as we rowed south back towards the estuary, Albi grabbed my arm and told me to look at the strand. On the dark shore there were faint flickers of firelight.

'That's him. It must be,' I said, turning the boat to land. 'Cover your head,' I told Albi, as the moon glanced off his white hair and made it glow like a beacon. He put up his hood and we bent to the oars, aiming to land a hundred strides north of the fire. We beached the boat without too much difficulty, hid it under driftwood and seaweed, then set off to spy on Vasser's jarl.

He sat with his back to us, tending the fire where a stew of shellfish bubbled over the flames. I put out a hand, warning Albi, drew my knife and crept forward. With my foot on the back of his cloak and my knee in the small of his back, I grabbed Einar's hair and pulled back his head, exposing his throat to my blade.

Einar's eyes flicked wide to mine.

'Berengeria,' he said hoarsely. 'Queen.'

I let him go.

'Einar,' I said.

Einar's eyes fixed on Albi. 'Who's this?' he said.

Albi answered him. 'Albinus. *Waes thu hael.*'

'Saxon?' Einar muttered.

'He's a friend,' I said quickly.

I pointed my blade at Einar.

'What are you doing here?' I said. 'And where's Vasser?'

CHAPTER 20
EINAR'S TALE

'Where is he?'
'Still in the south, but he will come, as sure as night follows day, now that Halfdan is dead—'

'*Halfdan? Dead?*' The king of the Jorvik stronghold, whom I had planned to make my friend.

'Yes. He was killed in Ireland. Did you not know? Vasser will come back to claim Jorvik for himself. He will try to claim the whole of the north for himself.'

'And you—whose side are you on?'

Einar hung his head, then slowly lifted it and said: 'Vasser holds my brother's life in his hands. You remember Trygg?' I nodded. Young fiery Trygg had once saved Snorri's life, when her leg had been caught in a vicious trap. 'I've longed to join you, believe me, only my fear for Trygg—'

'Do others feel as you do, among Vasser's jarls?'

'I'm sure of it. We were always warriors, invaders even, but Vasser has turned us into murderers—this was not the only holy place he has ravaged—and those who hesitated felt the prick of his sword. If I speak out, you must do all you can to protect Trygg. Vasser will kill him if he suspects that I have betrayed him.'

'I'll do what I can for Trygg and any who seek to leave Vasser's service. Speak, Einar.'

Einar studied the crashing waves. He lifted a handful of sand and slowly let it fall through his fingers.

'I *wanted* to keep you safe—'

'*Safe?*' My words erupted like lava. 'If I needed to be kept *safe*, I had my own jarls to call on.'

'Those were not Vasser's orders.'

'What then?' Einar's sheep eyes told me the truth and I could picture Vasser shouting it out for all to hear as he left for the south.

'This lot are all going to die of starvation—no Saxon will help them—but keep her safe for me, Einar! That's my bride I'm talking about!'

'Beren!' Our discussion broke off as Albi emerged from the cave, torch aloft. 'You must see this!'

I followed him into the cave.

Everywhere he had placed torches ablaze, casting dancing shadows to illumine my father's ship. Under a ragged canvas, stained with brine and silt, was *Swanwing*, my father's dragonship, the very same, with its finely carved and gilded prow. The very same that I thought we had set blazing, filling the sky with fire-arrows, until the ship with Thorkil's body was lost in a sheet of flame.

I leapt on board. 'Thorkil!' I ripped the gold shield aside to look again on my father's body, but where Thorkil had lain there was only a piece of old sail, thrown over a haphazardly piled heap of objects. I uncovered them and there lay a treasure fit for an emperor: thick gold, ingots of silver, rubies, emeralds, diamonds. Wrapped in a purple cloth was a Christian cross. I passed it to Albi.

'It's from St Bede's,' he said. Clasping the cross to his chest, he looked down at the treasure. 'It's all from St Bede's.'

Einar nodded. 'It's all there, everything that was taken.'

'In the spring raid?'

'Yes.'

Albi laid the cross aside. As he went on unpacking the treasure, I saw other things: my father's cloak and his gold-banded helmet, buckles and brooches, the death gifts that should have burned with his body.

I jumped down to face Einar. 'Where is my father's body? Where is Thorkil?'

'Thorkil's body was burnt, as you witnessed, but not on this ship. The rite was fulfilled. He rests at peace.'

'That he does not!' I paced to the cave entrance eager to breathe fresh air. 'I have seen his shadow soul. He sends his messenger, the fox. My father does not rest at peace.'

Albi came to me, but I turned away. I could bear no comfort. Hugging my arms tightly over my chest I stared at the sea. Then I heard Albi speak to Einar. I turned to listen. 'What ship was burnt? A replica?'

'Yes. Last winter, when *Swanwing* was in need of repair, Vasser took it to his own yard. There his carpenters added the final touches to its double; not exact, but good enough to pass as the original, at a distance, long enough for the rite to take place. That same night *Swanwing* was brought here, under canvas, by the most northerly route, where there was little chance of detection. It has remained hidden ever since.'

I went and ran my hand over the ship's side, as Einar went on. 'Vasser planned to be king. He acted the faithful brother at home, but abroad he cut a swathe through Thorkil's efforts to make peace with the Saxons. His nature is bloody and cruel, and in recent years it's grown worse. He revels in slaughter. We must stop him.'

My mind was full of darkness, as I recalled images from my childhood. Vasser making me a wooden sword to be a warrior. Lifting me onto his shoulders so that I could shield my eyes on a hot harvest day to look for Asa in the fields. Pouring the oil at Thorkil's crowning, making the invocation to mighty Othinn to keep his king-brother from harm.

Vasser the Liar.

'And the battle for the Mark?' I asked. 'Was that part of his plan?'

'Those who invaded the Mark were his allies. The Mark was his gift to them.'

'His *gift*? In return for what?'

'Untrammelled passage on the trade routes to the east. And Thorkil's death.'

Vasser the Traitor.

I stared at Einar. 'Who killed my father?'

White-faced he spilled out the truth.

'Vasser killed him. I was there.'

Vasser the Murderer.

My breath left me.

'What about Beren?' Albi said. 'Why did he not kill Beren? She is Thorkil's heir.'

'Vasser will take me as wife.' I blurted out the sour words. 'That I will *never* be!'

Albi spoke to Einar. 'Will you now join with Saxons to fight Vasser?'

Einar nodded. 'I should be glad to—it would ease my soul. I want to repay my debt.'

Turning abruptly away from me, he left the cave and hunkered down by the fire, casting a great piece of driftwood on to the embers.

I went to stand at the edge of the waves, letting the chill fret of the surf wash over my feet. Brine smell filled the air and I took deep breaths of it. Then Great Othinn swelled in my spirit and made me strong. I threw back my head, looked up to the stars, held my arms wide and shouted to the wind:

'Othinn! Othinn! Othinn! Hear my vow. I shall avenge my father's death. I shall stand against my father-brother, Vasser. Put your hand to mine and grant me his deathblow!'

As the wind tossed my words away, I waited for an answer. I heard only the crash of the surf. 'May Thorkil's spirit be at peace in the hall of warriors,' I whispered.

CHAPTER 21
BERENGERIA QUEEN

'You're late! I invite you to come fishing and you arrive late. What's your excuse?' Albi said, looking up briefly from the firepit on the riverbank, then settled another stone into its place on the rim. 'Lost your tongue? I don't believe it.'

With great care, he scraped away the dead grass all around so that the fire would not cross the barrier of stones and eat its way to the ditch and field behind us. 'Affairs of state, was it? Important discussions? Too important to share with a friend?'

Albi teased a smile from me, but I went on looking upriver, studying the current, as if it could tell me when Vasser and his warriors would arrive. Today it looked as peaceful a scene as it always did, without a hint of danger, the sun glinting on the sparkling waters, dippers watching the pools, darting, from time to time, to catch small fish for their supper. I was free to spend this time with my friend, but my mind was not free.

In the weeks following the discovery of Thorkil's ship, I had lived a halflife, caught in my thoughts like a drowning whale in a net. Boldly, on the strand, after hearing what Einar had to tell, I had called out: 'I shall stand against my father-brother! Grant me his death-blow!' But there's a gulf between making bold plans and putting them into action.

In clear daylight, I knew that for all our plans and preparations, we could not win a fight against Vasser, and, staring at catastrophe, I cursed myself for not understanding more, sooner. We had peace with the Saxons, but it would count as nothing if we lost our lives. Vasser had superior fighting strength, that's what it came down to. My uncle was an experienced warrior: I was untried. His warriors would be well-fed: mine were hungry. He was certain of his troops, knew all their strength and weaknesses: I knew my Viking companions, but I did not know the strength of the Saxon side.

'Keep your warriors ready—that is the price of freedom.'

Thorkil's words stung my thoughts. My army consisted of farmers, smiths, herdsmen, led by a handful of warriors. We could not hope to win the fight.

Albi tended the fire. 'When did you last eat?' I shook my head. Couldn't remember. My hand, slippery with sweat, fretted on the handle of my knife, safe in its sheath on my belt. It was a comfort to feel it there: I didn't want to let go. I swallowed hard, then moved closer to the fire and sat down in its light and heat.

'Oh.' The small gasp left my lips unbidden as I saw the pile of fish laid out at Albi's side under a layer of dock leaves. 'You're hungry?' I nodded and he set up a cooking frame, two branches set on either side of the fire, supporting an iron rod, on which he spitted a large fish.

'Watch that, will you, while I catch some more?'

The sun was low in the west. It would be dark soon.

'Wait for the dark,' I said. 'The fish will bite better.'

'You can speak then?' Albi said, lying flat on the riverbank with his nose almost touching the water.

'Strange fishing with no hook,' I said. Albi turned and wiggled his fingers, then went back to his 'fishing'. I shrugged and turned the spit. Dripping oil hissed in the flames.

'Sh!' Albi said. 'Nearly had one then!'

'If you catch a single fish by staring at it, I'll give you an armring.'

'I don't catch them by staring at them.' He beckoned me over. Where Albi was lying, the slow river pooled into a weedy bay. Albi held his hand loosely in the water. I dropped to my knees by his side.

'Don't come any closer! They'll see you.'

I leaned forward as far as I could without letting my reflection disturb the mirror-like surface. A pink-flushed spotted trout nudged Albi's fingers. A splash and a flurry, and Albi held the fish high in his hands. He rolled over, despatched it with a single blow and presented it to me.

'A gold armring, I think you said.'

'I said "staring" not "tickling"!'

'You pick nits worse than Anselm!' he said, but we both grinned and shouldered each other amiably as we went to sit by the fire.

Albi took the baked fish from the spit, broke it and passed half to me. The flesh was sweet and fresh. My mouth hurt, watering with the smell of it. I bit deeply into the fish.

' "O fish of little wit!" ' Albi sang, between mouthfuls. 'You'd think they'd learn. Here they sit in their nice calm pool, so stupid that they fall for the same trick every time. You'd think they'd learn to protect themselves. You'd think they'd at least avoid the pool. But no, back they come. Dimwits! The blow will fall. Death comes to the dimwits! They don't even put up a fight! Fight or die!'

Fury erupted in me, a red tide. I flung my fish away. 'Perhaps they know they can't win!'

'What?' Albi spun round in surprise.

The words spilled from me like a flood. 'We are like these fish! We can't win against Vasser. My tribe will be slaughtered. I can't save them.'

Albi turned on his knees and leaned forward to look at me. '*You* can't save them? The great Queen Berengeria can't save her tribe? Beren, listen to me. Look at me. There is no Queen Berengeria here. This isn't the Mark. The old ways are finished. You're not alone. We're all in this together and we'll fight together. This is a good land worth fighting for.

'No one expects you to win this fight on your own. Not your people, not us. Only *you*. But if you insist on carrying out your plan without our help, then I wish you well. If the time comes that you need us, then cross the river and come to the monastery.' He turned back to his fish. 'Everything's ready.'

It was a good plan. Faced with Vasser's superior

strength and numbers, I wanted to avoid a battle for as long as possible, certainly long enough to evacuate the camp and move all my people to safety within the bounds of St Bede's, and also to allow safe passage across the river to those of Vasser's men who wished to join us. The plan was to welcome Vasser and his warriors into the camp for the Winternight feast, as expected, plying them with ale until they were fast in sleep, then to remove their weapons. At sunrise the next day I would demand Vasser Wulf's life for the life of my father, and discover which of his warriors stood with us, who against. It was an honourable course of action—I could otherwise have poisoned Vasser with his first cup of ale—so why did my spirit shriek that it would fail?

'Everything's ready?' Albi repeated, this time asking a question.

'It is,' I replied. I got to my feet and went to stand at the river's edge. 'If I fail and it comes to a fight, I shall keep him busy for as long as I live—I shall not cross the river—you will have time—' My words stumbled and fell. It was a vain, silly boast. I frowned at the water.

'We have fighters to call on—Anselm has sent for the fyrd.'

'The fyrd?' I looked round. 'What's that?'

'Every man or woman within twenty miles, willing to fight. After the raid, it was decided that we would do all we could to defend the monastery against such another attack. The fyrd will come to Anselm's call.

They will come. If Vasser Wulf tries to ride roughshod over us, he will find that he cannot.' Albi began to gather his things. 'All you have to do, if it comes to it, is cross the river.' He slung his pack over his shoulder, then looked into my eyes. 'You don't have to do this alone.'

The sound of homecall rang out, then died away. Deep in thought, I gathered the fish into my pack as Albi kicked earth over the fire.

'What's that?' he said, peering at a hilltop far distant, down stream.

'Fire,' I said.

'It's the signal. They're coming.' Albi spoke calmly, but I was not calm. My hands shook as I watched the beacon fires lit, from one hilltop to the next, passing on the news of the arrival of Vasser and his warriors.

'I'll warn Cedd. We'll get everyone back to the monastery. God be with you—' Albi put his hand on my arm and I covered it with shaking fingers. 'Cross the river,' he repeated. 'If you have to. Don't leave it too late.'

CHAPTER 22
VASSER WULF

Vasser had already arrived when I got back to the settlement: I knew it, though he was nowhere to be seen. Brand stood stiffly with little Gerd as she filled a pail from the river, keeping an obvious lookout, and, as I rode into the heart of the camp, others silently appeared from their shelters to watch me pass. In answer to my unspoken question, Brokk gave a quick nod. *Vasser's here.*

Vasser's chief jarls had accompanied him. They were making themselves quite at home in the camp, cleaning their gear, quaffing ale, swapping idle chat with those who served them. Helga was in charge of this provender, sending Leif and Sigrid to fetch food and ale for the men, hay and water for the horses. None of my own people met my eyes.

By home shelter, I slid from Snorri's back, then, as I reached over her steaming hide to remove the damp saddlecloth, Vasser rode into camp from the seaward path and called out to me.

'Thor-kil's daughter!' His voice was slurred with scorn. *Ale-tongue*, I thought, as the words slipped sidewise from his mouth. *'Thor-kil's!'* Vasser gurgled with laughter like a blocked ditch. *'Daughter!'* His mockery of my

name announced that we were now enemies. In the little time since his return he had discovered that much. *So be it.* I swung round.

'I have my own name!' I thundered.

In his dark leather shirt and breeks, ornamented with silver, he looked so like a king, so like Thorkil, my father, that I caught my breath. Swaying astride his warhorse, Vasser looked down at me.

'Beren-ger-ia!' Vasser chewed the sounds of my name as if they were spoiled oats and, without thought, I put my hand to my knife. Vasser threw back his head and laughed until tears were streaming down into his beard. What use was my knife against the armoury he carried? He bristled with weapons: iron axe, iron-tipped spear on his back, war-helmet at his side, sword and knife at his waist.

'Beren-geria,' he repeated in a low voice. 'How do you find your new home? To your liking?' Vasser made an effort to control his loose speech. He dismounted and Sigrid stepped forward to take his reins. Without waiting for my approval, she turned Vasser's horse away for hay and fresh water. 'I hope you have plenty of fodder,' Vasser called out loud to the empty air, watching his horse until it was lost to view. He turned to shout orders. 'Prepare a feast! The men are home! The rest are coming. They're on their way. Ha.' It was a threat, meant to disarm me, but I stood my ground.

He growled and wiped spittle from the corners of his mouth. 'They'll be here in an hour. Lay out your best.

They are all weary.' Dropping heavily on to the bench outside the shelter, he called for ale. As Finn filled the ale-horn, Vasser watched my face. I stood inscrutable, as more and more of his warriors showed themselves, armed, standing among our tents.

The food arrived and I watched him eat. Afterwards he reached out to draw aside the doorcloth to the shelter and said, in a thick, oily voice, 'Where do you lay your head tonight, sweetheart?' He ran his rough forefinger down my cheek.

'No business of yours!' I retorted, knocking his hand away. Vasser looked into the shelter. 'Room for both of us,' he murmured.

'Only if you wish to die,' I replied, in a tone that would have shrivelled Othinn himself.

When Vasser laid his hand on my shoulder, I jerked back and spat at his feet. He made no further attempt to persuade me. He was about to step inside the shelter alone, when Asa appeared.

'My Lord Vasser, sit here,' she said, brushing aside dead leaves from the board outside the shelter, and laying down a precious haunch of roast boar. 'Surely you have room for a morsel.'

'Aye, and more than a morsel, Asa!' he said, digging his blade into the meat. 'Light some torches, there! These woods are dark places. Asa! Asa! Come and join me!'

'Surely, lord,' she replied. 'But first I must take the ale to your men.'

'Serve me first,' he said, holding out his empty cup.

Asa refilled her ale-horn from the barrel, and poured some out for him, which he emptied in a single draught. '*She* knows her *place*,' Vasser said to me.

'I am Thorkil's heir,' I said, stung beyond caution. 'My place is not as your slave. '

Like a well-greased spring, Vasser leapt up and clamped one hand to my throat. He unbent like a bow, to lift me bodily into the air, and though I kicked and pummelled him with hard fists, my eyes swam as his iron fingers crushed my jaw.

'Thorkil is dead,' he whispered. 'His *word* is dead. Say it.' He threw me to the ground, where I crouched on all fours, choking the breath back into my body.

'Never,' I croaked. I was gathering myself to lunge upwards, when I caught Asa's signal. Behind Vasser, she shook her head, and laid her finger to her lips.

Helga appeared, with Sigrid. 'This way, lord,' Helga said, distracting Vasser, while Sigrid helped me up, covertly signing to me to let things be. 'There is a glade in the wood, lord, with a fresh water spring and a pool for bathing,' Helga was saying. 'It has been softened with lavender flowers.'

'I thank you,' Vasser growled. 'And for my men?'

'For all of you.'

As he went to follow Helga to the glade, he turned and threw his knife, and it landed at my feet, its steely point stuck in the earth. I snatched it up.

'You shall be Wulf's queen,' he said quietly.

'Nev—' Asa cut off my retort with a sharp kick to my ankle and pushed in front of me. As Vasser turned away she laid her hand firmly on mine, to prevent me from throwing his own knife into his back.

'Let him go,' she hissed, smiling and smiling, while Vasser left us. I wished my stare had been fire arrows burning into my uncle's flesh.

When all was quiet again, Asa pulled me aside. 'Vasser knows that you will stand against him. He could give the order to kill us at any time. We must leave now!'

'The weapons?'

'No time. We must cross the river!'

Like wraiths, Brand and Einar stepped out of the trees and bowed their heads to me.

'We have had no opportunity to speak to Vasser's men,' Brand said. 'He sees everything!'

'And they are afraid of him,' Einar added. 'But I have spoken to Trygg and he will take his chance, as soon as he may, to leave Vasser and join us. Tyr waits for us at the cave. Almost everything has now been taken to safety—there are one or two last things to collect. There's nothing to be done about the ship, but at least the treasure will be safe.'

I nodded. 'Go quickly then. Make sure nothing is left. You've put Thorkil's possessions on one side? I want them saved.' Brand gave a quick nod. 'It's well, then,' I said.

More 'wraiths' appeared from the wood. Brokk, Arn, and little Gerd. They all carried packs and weapons, as if prepared for a journey.

'Tell them to go!' Asa said.

'Brokk?' I said, asking him for his opinion.

'Asa's right. We should all cross the river. Vasser is too strong for us. Did you hear him say there are more warriors on the way? It's foolish to stay here and die. We cannot stand against them, not alone. I say we go now and set up camp there. And that's where we shall fight and take a stand if we have to, with the river between us.'

'Go then, quickly,' I said. 'Cross the river. Take the others and let Father Anselm know.'

'And you?'

'I shall stay and keep watch here, to count how many warriors arrive in the night. Then, at sunrise, I shall face Vasser alone. No, Brokk—' As my companion offered to stay with me, I waved him away. 'It is my duty and my right. With the help of great Othinn, though it cost me my life, I shall make Vasser pay, if only with a single cut of my blade, the debt he owes for my father's death. Your task is to guard the others. Now—go!'

Leif and Sigrid came from the glade to refill their alehorns. 'All is well,' Sigrid murmured. 'They're already half-drowned in ale-sleep.'

'We'll make sure then—' said Asa. She took a couple of pinches of some powdery herb from a small cloth bag tucked into her belt, and added them to the ale. 'Something to make their rest even more peaceful,' she said.

'Not death,' I said, shaking my head. 'I would have them live. They may yet join us.'

'Not death. Just a long peaceful sleep,' Asa replied, as she rubbed her fingers and tucked the bag back into her belt.

CHAPTER 23
I SEE A SIGN

Dawn came at last, in a grey haze hanging low over the river. Asa had worked secretly, with the others, throughout the night, to take what remained of our gear across to the Saxon side. She was the last to leave, with Skar, on his final crossing to transport the hawks to safe harbour at the monastery. I asked him to leave Raed with me. Raed and I would face Vasser together.

I made my way down the path and went to stand at the edge of the water. Vasser was still asleep, in the home shelter, which I had been obliged to give up to him, choosing, myself, to sleep with the horses.

Twice, during my sleepless night, I had gone in to finish him. He had lain, like a sodden sack of grain, with his head thrown back and his red throat, bristly as a hedgepig, naked to my blade. Twice I was tempted, but I stayed my hand. I was no skulking assassin dealing death in the dark. When the time came to kill Vasser, as it surely would, Othinn would guide me.

In spite of the danger of Vasser waking and discovering how we had tricked him before I was ready, I took the time to put on battle dress: leather breeks, linen shirt, leather tunic and belt. On both forearms I wore strong hide bracers. My pack of darts and bow were slung over my right shoulder, my sword and axe in my belt. My knife, the gift of my father Thorkil, lay safe there too, straight across my middle, its hilt within swift reach of my hand. Finally I was ready.

I climbed on to Snorri's back and felt strong and proud. I wanted Vasser, stumbling down to the river bank, in his half-sleep, holding up his breeks, intent only on voiding his bowels, to find me there, waiting. All Asa's urging could not make me flee. When I defied him and his warband, I would look Vasser straight in the eye as his equal. It was the test I set myself as leader. I was no lurker, no walker in shadows. Vasser had issued his challenge and I would answer it boldly in clear terms, so that there was no misunderstanding. I was leader here. This was my territory. These were my people. To secure peace for them I must fight Vasser, to the death, if need be.

I have my own blood debt to claim. Vasser will pay for the murder of Thorkil.

A vision struck me, of Vasser, my father-brother, killed by me as a traitor and so condemned to wander for ever the dark, echoing halls of the shameful dead. I shuddered. I must crush all thoughts of pity. He had shown none to me, none to Thorkil. I must steel myself to the deed.

On the riverbank, in the early mist, I waited. Raed anxiously kneaded my left shoulder, eager to fly. I held firm to the thongs tied to her legs and passed her the morsels of meat Skar had left, which I had tucked into my belt. She tugged at them gratefully, tilting her throat to swallow them whole.

Downriver, during the night, more ships had arrived. They had been tied together, side to side, forming a ship bridge to give the warriors an easy route shore to shore. I watched the men wake from their ale-sleep and light up their breakfast fires. The sound of their calls, farts, and belches broke the silence of the now empty settlement. Some splashed in the river, sluicing the sleep away. Others, from ingrained habit, examined gear and tackle, for splinters or frayed ends. They tugged at the sails and pulled hard on the ropes that bound the ships in the row, each to each, making the bridge secure. They didn't seem to fear any oncoming battle.

I looked to the far shore, past the signs of our fresh camp: stands of spears poking above brushwood hides, piles of darts ready to hand, and Brokk and Brand standing guard. I could see where the track which led into the wood and then to the Saxon village, branched off to the Hill and the coast, and, beyond, to the safe harbour of the monastery. I had expected company, if not to take part in my fight, at least to observe its outcome, but the road and the wood lay empty, sunlit, peaceful. My heart shivered. Half-closing my eyes, I squinted at possible hiding-places, behind rocks, dunes, among trees. No one was there. Nothing moved. There was no glint of steel to betray the weapon of a Saxon warrior. If Vasser cut me down,

I prayed that Anselm would arrive in time to save my tribe.

In the next breath, Vasser came striding down the path from the settlement, fully dressed in battle gear, but weaponless. He was tying the tags of his wrist-guard. I turned Snorri to face him.

'What's this, Thorkil's daughter? No ale-horn to greet me with? No bread? No groats? No word of welcome for your lord?'

'No lord of mine,' I said. Vasser looked down to finish his task, as if he had not heard.

I faced him, Raed on my shoulder, my right hand crooked ready to draw my sword, and, in as bold a voice as I could muster, I issued my challenge.

'Vasser Wulf. I claim a blood debt for the death of my father, Thorkil. You will pay me for his death.'

Vasser glanced up at me and roared with laughter. Behind him, from between the tents of the empty camp, his hearthjarls now gathered, silently, at his back. I was wrong to think he would meet me in single combat.

On my shoulder Raed picked up her feet, kneading my flesh. Lazily she stretched one wing, then the other, preparing to fly on my command.

'Should I let you live for that insult, Thorkil's daughter? I think not.'

The speed of Vasser's attack took me by surprise. As a spear, thrown on his signal by one of his men, whistled past my ear and splashed into the river, Raed threw herself into the air and I let her go. As Vasser lunged at me, I slipped from Snorri's back and drew my sword.

Vasser was too strong for me. His first hacking blow to my right forearm rendered it nerveless and my weapon dropped from my frozen fingers. He kicked it out of reach. As he stepped back, I managed to draw my bow, but as if the bones in my hand had melted, I fumbled to nock the dart, which dropped at my feet. Vasser's warriors began to laugh and beat their thighs with their fists.

Then as the blood surge filled my body and I rushed at Vasser to grapple with him, the laughter stopped. I knew Vasser was too strong, so my tactic was to close with him, forcing him to hold me in his arms, in mock-embrace, until I gained an advantage. Vasser still had not drawn his blade. He treated me with contempt. Strong in wrestling, he forced me to my knees. Some of his men, not sensing the seriousness of the contest, began to call out to me, 'Berengeria! Thorkil's daughter! Get up! Fight! Fight!'

Either they had not heard my challenge or, hearing, had dismissed it, seeing this fight as an entertaining spat between warriors. Then, as Vasser relieved me of my last weapons, my silver axe and my knife, and began to deliver hard blows to my body with his closed fist, some tried to stop him. They were kicked away for their pains, but as Vasser turned from me to deal with them, I had respite. Vasser's hold on me lessened and I toppled like a felled tree.

As if I were already beaten, I lay on the ground, using the time to catch breath. Under my brow I glanced at the river, gauging how far I had to walk to reach it. I was no coward but no simpleton either. The wise man falls back, all the better to jump forward.

As Vasser's jarls disputed the rules of the fight, attempting to laugh him out of continuing, I noted the thrust of his jaw and the white knuckles of his tightly closed fist and saw how it swayed at his side, like a hammerhead. Vasser would not let me go. There was the smell of the raid on him, the blood lust. It lived in him, like a beast. Only spilled blood would fill its maw.

And I must live, to fight on. Grabbing Snorri's rein, I dragged myself to the river. I saw my knife lying there in the muddy bank, Othinn's gift. I retrieved it and got to my feet. Then I put my knife back in my belt and led Snorri into the water.

I kept going and my back pricked with the expectation of the sting of dart or spear. None came. Then a sound came to me, of a hundred people breathing, shifting, chinking weapons, clearing throats.

On the opposite shore, lining the bank, were the people of this territory: Cedd and his Saxons, Asa, Brand and our Viking tribe, each and every one armed and ready to fight.

As I waded a little further, a rank of warrior-priests on horseback trotted out of the wood and stood behind them. Albi and Father Anselm made their way through the company and came to take up position, either side of the ford.

'Keep going!' Albi shouted. 'Keep going!'

I looked back to see Vasser's jarls, puzzled, draw

their swords. Vasser held out his arm to them, so that none made move to stop me as I waded into the deepest part of the river. Perhaps they could not believe their own eyes, that their Viking brothers and sisters now faced them as enemies, arrows nocked, spears at the ready, alongside Saxons.

In the middle of the river, in the slow-moving current, I stopped and looked up into the now blue cloudless sky, my attention caught by a hawk's call. At treetop height, Raed, her familiar bow shape, dark in the sky, hovered over me. Some of the crowd looked up and gasped. In disbelief, that she took stand there for so long? A fixed mark, a dark cross, over my head? Or was it belief?

Some crossed themselves. 'It's a sign,' they murmured. '*A sign . . . a sign . . .* '

When I had safely reached the other side of the river, I saw that Raed had gone. Still under the gaze of Vasser and his warriors, I was warmly greeted by Albi and Anselm. I saw Vasser give the signal to let me go. His men lowered their weapons.

'*A sign . . .* what sign do they mean?' I asked.

Leading me into the crowd, on to the road back to the monastery, Albi explained.

'Jesus the Christ waded into the river and God sent the bird to hover over him in the same way, saying, *"This is my Son, in whom I am well pleased."* I suppose the people thought God might be choosing you too.'

My blood rose to my cheeks. Surely not. It didn't seem the sort of thing Othinn would bother with. Nevertheless I was curious.

'Was the bird a hawk?'

'No, a dove. A dove for peace.'

'What does a hawk signify?'

'War. It signifies war.'

Whether from the Jesus God or from Othinn, Raed's stand was a sign of war. But Vasser left us alone to retire that day, and that evening we held moot, all of us together, within the monastery walls.

CHAPTER 24
AN UNEXPECTED VISITOR

We held moot in the refectorium, and, like all warriors on the eve of battle, drank deeply to our success, passing the ale-horn each to each along the board. Father Anselm sat at its head. I sat at his right hand with Albi next to me. On his left sat Tyr, then Brokk and Helga. Next came Asa, Sigrid, and Leif. Cedd sat opposite Anselm, at the other end of the board.

Making up the remaining places were monks from St Bede's. I nodded a greeting to Lucius and Titus. Two others sat with them, their heads bowed as if to study the grain in the wood of the board. Behind us, along the walls, stood Einar, Trygg, and Finn, with the rest of the Saxons, as many as could attend. Brand and Arn stayed by the river with some of Father Anselm's men. The general mood of the assembly was cautious, with the Saxons covertly eyeing us and our weapons. I must do all I could to win their trust.

Father Anselm called us to order, holding high a plain bull's horn which served as moot-horn to signal the turn of each speaker. After words of welcome, he spoke to the Saxons: 'Are the weapon pits full?'

As he laid down the horn, there was a silence as if

none wanted to be the first to give answer. Then, under Anselm's sharp gaze, one replied, 'Full to overspill. With no harvest to gather, what else have we had to spend time on, besides making weapons? We have seaxes and arrows, spears and shields, but not enough hands to wield them. It's warriors we need.'

As he laid down the horn, I took it up.

'We are here now,' I said. 'We will fight with you.' I looked boldly along the row of Saxon faces, but all averted their eyes and stayed silent. 'There are no words which will bring back your dead,' I said, 'nor ours either. But we can make recompense of a kind for the Viking raid.' I reached into my pack and took out the gold cross which had been stolen by Vasser. Amid gasps and surprised cries as they came forward to look, I set it down, with due reverence, in the middle of the board. 'All that was taken will be returned to you. I have found the spoils that Vasser Wulf took from St Bede's. My men have toiled long to bring the treasure here from its hiding place, and now wait outside to hand it back for safe keeping within the monastery.' At this, Father Anselm signalled to the two monks, who, gathering a handful of men to help them, left to attend to the treasure. When they had gone, he seized the horn.

'With this deed, Beren has shown good faith and a most generous spirit. It's up to us now to show ours in return. Hear what she has to say.' As he resumed his seat, I began to speak.

'We will fight with you, against Vasser Wulf. He is enemy to both of us—'

'Fine words,' Cedd blurted out, 'but talk is no good against swords! How many warriors stand with him? What is his strength?'

'I will not deceive you,' I said, nodding to Brokk to give his report.

'Almost eighty warriors, all hardened in battle, fully armed.'

There was an anxious outcry at this, with calls of *'It's hopeless!'* and *'We'll all be killed!'*, *'How can we stand against such a force?'* in the midst of which Anselm's voice rose, like a fount of clear water. 'Peace! Calm yourselves.'

As the company subsided, I again took the horn.

'Einar, who has brought back the treasure, tells me there are those of Vasser's men who seek to leave him. They are sick of war and would live in peace. It will be hard for them to leave their master, but I believe we should welcome them.' I waited but none spoke, so I went on. 'Only the gods know whether we shall survive the battle, but I know this: when Vasser Wulf comes here, I and my people will be here to meet him. We shall stand to look in his eyes. We shall not run from him and his force.' I paced the hall, walking behind the seated company, locking stares with those silently crowding the walls. 'Vasser Wulf has committed great injuries here, at the monastery and in the village. He has brought death to your kinsmen. He owes a debt for those lives and he shall be made to pay. We shall make Vasser pay! I shall fight not only for myself, but for all of us! To make a peace for all of us!'

At this, my own people gave a great shout. Still Cedd and the Saxons stayed silent. What more could I do? I resumed my place at the board.

Then Einar took up the ale-horn and went to refill Cedd's cup.

'What say you?' he said. 'Do you still fear the word "Viking"? Can we not bury our differences and fight Vasser together?'

'Einar is right.' Father Anselm laid both hands flat on the board. 'If we keep up this war, more men and women will die. What good is that? We need people, not corpses—people to live here and work the land. Beren's people are healers and makers, sailors and traders. We need them. We are ready to fight.

'Last spring Vasser Wulf taught us a lesson and we learnt it well. This time he will not find it so easy to take the monastery. It is well-defended, with full stores of food, water, and weapons. We have warriors here, Saxon and Viking—what matter the name if the heart and the will is the same? And there are more on the way. I have called up the fyrd. Every able-bodied man and woman within twenty miles will come to our aid. Together we can defeat Vasser Wulf.'

'How can we trust Vikings?' A man's voice, deep and powerful, called from the doorway. Cedd and Brand drew their blades, as a cloaked stranger approached the board. 'Peace!' the stranger called and held his arms wide to show that he was unarmed. When he threw back his hood, I got to my feet, alerted by Father Anselm's stifled exclamation—'My lord!'

'How can we trust Vikings?' the stranger repeated. 'That is the question and the sticking-point.' As a ripple of surprise ran through the Saxons, as they began to fall on one knee and bow their heads in allegiance, as Cedd stood and also bowed, I went to look for myself into the face of Aelfred, the Saxon king.

His eyes were as grey as slate, with a most searching look. He stood not much taller than I, and he smiled as I studied his expression, and stood his ground without moving. His cheeks were briar-scratched and mud-flecked, his hair tangled. Even so, here stood a king.

'How can we trust you?' he repeated, as I now gave him the bow of peace.

'*Waes thu hael*, Aelfred Cyning,' I replied. 'I did not expect to meet you here.'

'Anselm sent word when you arrived. You are Aelswyn's daughter.'

Shock stole my breath, then I said, foolishly, 'Aelswyn was my mother's name.'

'Yes. She was my mother's most constant friend. Osburga was stricken with a lasting grief when Aelswyn died.'

Again I bowed, acknowledging this compliment to the mother I knew only in name. Aelfred glanced to the end of the board. 'The loss of your sister was a sorrow to us all, Anselm.'

I swung round.

'Your sister?'

'Yes.' Anselm's eyes smiled at me. 'I had thought there would be a time, later perhaps, to talk to you about your mother, and your father's visits here, to woo her and persuade her to marry him and live with him as queen, in the Mark. Vasser never got over losing her.'

'Vasser?'

'The rivalry between Vasser and Thorkil was intense. But your mother chose Thorkil.'

'And that's why Vasser murdered him,' Einar said.

'Murder?' Aelfred moved to sit at the board and accepted the cup of ale that was passed to him.

'As good as,' Einar said, settling to tell Aelfred the story of how Thorkil died. And, as the company heard the tale of our defeat and voyage into exile, and finally understood that we too, my people and I, had suffered a great wrong at the hands of Vasser Wulf, I felt the mood change. Kind looks were exchanged, cups refilled, and the company seemed to move closer together, as if, in sharing our grief, the unseen barriers that had kept us apart were now melting like pack ice in the spring.

All eyes, Saxon and Viking, were on Aelfred Cyning, as if we waited for him to set seal on our plan.

'You will settle things with your uncle?' Aelfred said quietly when the tale was told and he knew that the treasure of St Bede's had been returned.

'I shall try, to my last breath. I swear it.' I replied, then before I spoke my next words, I looked along the board, and along the walls, at the faces of my people. 'Afterwards, after tomorrow's battle, when Vasser Wulf is dead, our whole wish is to live here in peace, to make this place our home.'

'Anselm?' Aelfred looked for Anselm's agreement and when the gesture was given, he took up the ale-horn and filled my cup. 'Fill your cups,' he said, raising his own to the company. 'Drink with me, to the strength of this alliance. Fight for the right and may God be on your side!'

'You came alone?' I asked, as we finished the first of several toasts.

'Guthrum thinks I'm still in the southern fens, but a cloaked traveller, with only one or two companions, may yet roam the land unaccosted.'

'I believe it is many days' ride from the fens,' I said. 'What brought you here? You did not come solely to meet Aelswyn's daughter.'

'Not that alone. King Halfdan of Jorvik is dead. The balance of power is disturbed. Who now strives to take his place? Raider or settler? I must find out what I can. I don't yet have the forces to fight both here in the north and in the south. Until that day comes, I must travel the land and learn every stride of it. How else will I discover who is my friend, who my enemy? How else know this country, in all its shapes and forms? Make no mistake, one day it will be one land, under one king.'

'Saxon or Dane?' I said pricked by the fear that this king was in the grip of greed, like Vasser Wulf, and intended, for all his fine words, to seize the land for himself.

'Only Almighty God knows the answer. One thing is certain: we must end the terror wrought by such as

Vasser Wulf. We have been at war too long. Too many people have died. Our trees are cut down to make ships and weapons, but we need them to build shelters and farmsteads. Every man, woman, and child must have his home and grain in the barn.'

'Only ravens smile at the sight of the slain,' said Father Anselm, coming to join us.

Over the rim of my cup, I watched the king. Could I trust *him*? Was there a band of his Saxon thegns waiting in the woods to kill us as we left?

'Are you here to get rid of us?' I asked. 'Are my people still savage Danes from across the sea? Am I your enemy?'

Aelfred laughed and shook his head. 'Your Viking blood does not make you so. Only greed and cruelty, murder and theft, would make you that. Berengeria, Aelswyn's daughter, you are welcome to settle here.'

As he got to his feet and raised his cup, all fell silent.

'I come to the moot to speak my mind. If you will listen, this is what I propose.' He gave pause, waiting to see who would raise their voice, but, as he turned to speak publicly to me, none spoke against him.

'Beren, Aelswyn's daughter, I shall not fight you and your people for this territory. My war is in the south. If you can live here, in peace with your Saxon neighbours, you will earn God's blessing and mine.' He raised his cup to me. 'We need strong leaders in this land, of whatever creed, to hold the peace for all of us.' Aelfred drank, so did I, then he said, addressing the whole company: 'The southern war is almost done, and, when I am ready, I shall forge an agreement with Guthrum. I might even make a Christian of him!'

At the thought of Guthrum turning Christian we all laughed out loud, a great belly laugh, which echoed to the rafters of the refectorium and out through the smokehole, into the night beyond.

'And Vasser Wulf?' I said, walking to the door with the king, as the laughter died away.

'He is your challenge. Great sins lie heavy on his soul. I shall pray for both of you.'

'What help can you give us?'

'I fear, none. I am here with two companions only. My main force stays to hold Guthrum at bay. Anselm,' he called, 'you have sent for the fyrd?'

'I have, my lord.'

'Then God speed.'

Aelfred had his hand on the door, then turned again.

'Anselm, how many now read and write?'

'Ten, lord.'

'Keep them to it. Write everything down. The scop's tales may fall into disuse, the songs die with the singer, but a writing may last for ever.' An icy blast cooled my cheeks, as he opened the door. Without looking back, he swept through it. Aelfred Cyning had gone.

'It seems we have his blessing,' Anselm said.

'Yes,' I said, 'and I am glad of it.' Slowly I turned to look at him. 'We are kin,' I said softly.

'Indeed we are, sister-daughter,' was the reply.

CHAPTER 25
THE LAST BATTLE

Vasser's man shouted his lord's request to us, that we should delay the fight until the next day, when he would lead his force to battle, for rule of the whole territory, 'to bring this parcel of land, the village and monastery under Viking Law, as was fitting, considering Vasser Wulf as the next King of Jorvik, Halfdan's successor, and Guthrum's man in the north.' I made formal reply to this, granting Vasser's request, though secretly I smiled at the idea that my uncle would be anyone's 'man'.

'He makes us wait, so that his men may refresh themselves,' grumbled Brand.

'It gives us more time to prepare,' I said. 'Brute strength and weapons will not win this fight. We have to use the fox's cunning.'

With this in mind, our first stratagem was to divide Vasser's forces with an attack on the ships. When he dispatched men to save them, our archers would pick them off on the river bank, one by one.

The rest we would draw deep into our territory, across the river and back to the monastery, where we planned further stratagems.

So all that day we used the time well, to set our

traps, to make more darts, sharpen more spears, while Father Anselm prepared beds and poultices for the wounded.

As dawn broke the next day, we faced Vasser and his men, each force lined up on opposite sides of the river.

Vasser stood at the front of his jarls, all armed with spears or swords, their helmeted faces stone grim. In the trees behind him stood more warriors, hidden. His whole troop was now a hundred, yet there were perhaps only thirty lined up on the bank: he came confidently to meet us with a token force only.

On their left arms the jarls carried shields, sharp-edged, which at a word they would lock together, each sliding under the rim of the next man's to form an impenetrable wall behind which they would push forward, blocking our spears and darts. Thirty could fell a hundred in that way, forcing them back, lifting the shield when they came face to face with their enemy, to stab a deathblow to the inner thigh. I had seen that. The blood gushes out like a stream. The wall was a deadly weapon and when Vasser gave the word, his men would not falter.

Upriver, his ship bridge held fast, the vessels' sides creaking and knocking together in the steady current. They seemed abandoned, though I knew they were not. How many warriors lay there in wait, ready to stream on to the Saxon bank, mounting a flank attack on Vasser's signal?

Albi was making his way to the bridge of ships,

with Brand and Helga. He had waved aside all my suggestions for the attack, insisting on some plan of sabotage, which he would not reveal. Only, he said, to those who might know the term, that he would use firepowder. There was no time to prise the secret recipe out of him: I must trust to his courage. Great Othinn grant him success.

The timing of Albi's attack was crucial. If successful, the diversion would stop Vasser's advance stone dead, in the middle of the river. It would divide his force.

'Stand firm,' I said, as Vasser's men, poised to attack, swayed in front of us, like wheat in a breeze. 'Steady.' I could hear Einar's breathing on my right. Tyr stood on my left.

Behind us, Cedd and Brokk, with the others from both settlements, stood side by side, with what weapons they could find: knives, swords, spears, sickles, scythes, rakes. At the rear stood the youngest, with piles of stones and sharp sticks. Their orders were to retreat to the monastery if the first ranks fell.

'Berengeria Thorkilsdatter!' Vasser's booming voice made the crows lift from the trees. They fluttered and swarmed above his head like the Valkyrie. His voice already carried the sound of victory. There was no breath of wind to lessen it; all heard his swagger. I drew my sword.

'Come to your master, Berengeria,' Vasser shouted. 'Obey your lord.'

'*You* come to me, Vasser Wulf! Death-dealer! Pay me for the life of Thorkil.'

Vasser moved his hand in a signal. His men stepped forward and locked shields.

'Will you face the wall, Beren?' he said. 'You and these—' he made a dismissive gesture. Cedd roared and lunged forward, but Einar put out his arm and held him back from entering the river.

'Pay for my father's life!' I called.

'And for my father's life! And for my mother's life and for the lives of my brothers!' shouted Cedd. Other Saxons echoed the shouts.

Vasser sneered, then stood aside to let the shield wall pass.

'Hold fast!' I shouted as the wall of men came towards us. I signalled to the bowmen sitting high in the trees behind us. They had strict orders: to fire only when they were sure of a target and to waste no arrows on the wall. Once battle was joined, and the wall broken, their vantage point would come into its own.

Vasser's men advanced to the middle of the river as if it were dry land, keeping the wall true and strong. They could have dealt great damage with their first throw of spears, but in their pride they expected to defeat us through terror. *Albi* . . . I breathed. *Now, Albi* . . . *Now!* The shield wall came on. I held my breath as a stillness fell over us. *Now! Albi* . . . *now!*

A blast went up from the ship bridge. And another. And a third. 'Hold fast!' I shouted as the shield wall began to falter, Vasser's men torn between advancing and looking to their ships. Booooomm . . . A fourth blast, the loudest, rent the air. As rigging and sails, broken spars and oars flew up in a cloud of destruction, then landed in the now bubbling river, the shield wall broke. Booooommm—a fifth blast, the greatest, settled it. As the middle ships of the bridge flew apart, Vasser's men did not wait to be told, but dropped shields and weapons. They ran back, yelling and cursing in the swelling current, then, joined by the men in the woods, made for their ships.

I ran up the slope for a better view. Two ships lay broken, the others adrift and banging into each other in the gurgling current, tied only by fraying ropes which could break at any moment. Vasser's men, scrambling on board or wading thigh-deep in the river, struggled to save them.

Cursing his men, Vasser himself gave a mighty roar and plunged into the river, laying into those who had stayed, a dozen or so, with the flat of his sword, forcing them into a ragged line. He came on to attack us alone, his sword raised to deliver a crushing blow. I rushed down the slope to prevent any from meeting his challenge.

'Back!' I called. 'Back! Go back!' Then, without looking at Vasser, I also turned from the river and fell back with the others.

Albi, Helga, and Brand joined us in front of the monastery gates. Smoke-reek covered them and I sent Brand with Helga straightway to find food and water.

As Albi and I hugged the breath from each other, I smelled the bitter scent of pitch in his hair.

'Send this firepowder back to where it came from,' I laughed. 'It's a weapon that stinks!' When Albi made no joking response, I pulled back. Then I saw the burns on his hands and the way they trembled, though he stuck them under his armpits out of sight. 'This fire—' I said.

'—is not for the unwary!' Albi said, grinning. But his grin was too wide, like that of a skull.

'Go and see to your hands. Find Anselm,' I said.

'But the battle—'

'—will wait. What good is a weapon without strong hands to wield it? Go to Anselm.'

'Don't start without me,' Albi said, hurrying away.

We hurriedly took up position in two lines, with our backs to the monastery, in front of the gates. On top of the fence, either side of the gates, armed monks stood at ward.

In the fields behind the monastery, stood the ranks of the fyrd, the common people of the territory, finally arrived, come at Anselm's request. Their first band was eighty strong. Others were on their way. Einar was with them, riding a stocky pony, with a small party of Saxon horsemen.

I sat astride Snorri, some distance from the first line, and waited for Vasser. I did not have to wait long, before he and his men came to stand fifty paces in front of me, armed with spear and shield, along the edge of the open ground.

Vasser had abandoned the shield wall. Braving the darts from our archers, he and his men had come on foot across the river, to meet us openly. Now they spread out, each man holding his two paces of land, as if to battle practice, not to face death at an enemy's hands.

When Vasser drew his sword and stepped forward, I again threw out my challenge. 'Vasser Wulf! No uncle of mine! You will pay the blood debt you owe me!'

Vasser's face swelled with menace. In fury, he brandished his sword. 'Why do you fight me, Thorkil's daughter? Are you not Viking? Wulf's queen, I would say.'

I thought of my forces, Viking and Saxon alike, and remembered our moot and the face of Aelfred, the Saxon king, the Christian, who would cede me land here to buy peace for all of us.

'Thorkil's daughter I am!' I shouted, and Othinn granted me breath to make my voice strong and sure. 'And Aelswyn's!' Vasser started at the sound of that name. 'I stand here for the honour of my Viking father—the father you killed! And in the name of my Saxon mother! Their two bloods mix in my veins! So be it! Take heed, Vasser Wulf! You will pay your debt here, with your blood! And afterwards Vikings and Saxons will hold the land in peace for any who will join us.' Vasser watched me, but made no answer.

'I have not yet drawn weapon against you!' I called to his men. 'Throw your weapons down. Decide for yourselves! You can end this now! Stand against bloodshed. Stand against murder. We can end the slaughter, here and now.'

Vasser snatched a spear from his henchman and threw it. But Othinn was with me and it fell short by six paces. I held my position and Vasser's face grew dark as a thundercloud. He turned to his men.

'We are the Viking terror! The hammer of Thor!' He swung his shield round and began to beat on it with the hilt of his sword. 'Wulf's men . . . Wulf's men . . . Wulf's men . . .'

Trained to this cry, his men took up the chant, beating its rhythm on their shields, stilling their fear to the sound of it as they prepared to launch their attack. Hearing the battle chant, others now streamed to join them from the river and wood, leaving the camp and the broken ships, coming to join final battle. There were many more than a hundred. Who were they? Where were they coming from?

I signalled my warriors to get ready. They drew their swords. Those inside the monastery nocked darts and lifted spears. Vasser's men raised their shields and stood, restive, waiting for the signal to move forward. Einar's horse, moving along the line of the fyrd, whinnied and reared. *Not yet.*

'Hold fast!' I murmured. 'Hold fast!' then, as Vasser's hand gave the signal—'NOW!' I yelled. *'NOW!'*

As a volley of spears flew again and again over my head, I turned and galloped hard for the monastery gates, which opened to receive us, falling back with my forces, as planned, drawing Vasser into our trap. The monks had laboured well, digging deep ditches in the open ground, filling them with brushwood and rocks, so that, to strangers, they looked part of the natural terrain. Some of Vasser's men noted them and tried to jump over, dismissing them scornfully as a childish defence, until they stumbled into the stinking pit of foul water beneath. None laughed then. And they howled loud and long when they found the sides slick with grease and impossible to climb.

Vasser crossed the ditches unharmed. Though for the present I stood safe on the monastery fence, when Vasser approached I drew my sword. Escaping all darts and spears, as if protected by a shieldcharm, he strode to the foot of the fence. He looked up at me.

'Why do you draw all these others into the fight? Why do you risk their lives?'

'I could ask you the same!' I replied. I looked past him to where his men, under constant fire from our archers and spearmen, were now dragging their comrades from the ditches and marching forward, under their shields.

'More march to join me, Beren! They know Halfdan is dead! There is land to seize—Saxon villages and monasteries to plunder!' He laughed at his own coarse and cruel joke.

'Einar has joined us!' I shouted, as much to his men as to Vasser. 'And young Trygg!' As they arrived within range, a volley of darts landed among them and several of his men fell, their shields and swords dropping from them, like discarded bones after a feast. 'Stop this!' I called.

'You could stop it now, Berengeria!' he shouted. 'This fight is between the two of us alone.' *Why did he say this now? Why had he not answered my challenge before, when he had the chance? What trick was he playing?*

'To claim this so-called blood debt you must face me, warrior to warrior. If you win, I shall leave this place never to return. I shall take my force back to the real fight, against Aelfred the Saxon. Guthrum waits for me. Face me alone, Thorkil's daughter. Or dare you not?'

I knew from his breathing and his stiff jaw that his blood was full. I also knew, trick or not, that I must face him.

I stepped up on to the fence, found my balance, then jumped. I landed heavily, recovered and sprang at Vasser. 'For Thorkil!' I shouted, giving a mighty blow. After that there was no more shouting.

Vasser was strong-armed, battle-hard, but I was quick on my feet. Othinn would decide the outcome.

Time stalled as the bloodsurge came on me and bathed me in Othinn's fire. I knew there were warriors all around us, shouting, as Saxons streamed out of the monastery to join battle. I knew when Einar rode to the fight, leading the men of the fyrd, to deal blows with hayfork and scythe. I saw fists raised and the flash and fall of blades, but it was none of my business. My eyes were fixed on Vasser's sword and I heard only the ding and dint of the iron as we traded blows, edge to edge.

The knock of his blade jarred my bones, then, with a knock of my own, I caught the top of his sword arm and a line of blood oozed from the wound. For reply Vasser drew his knife and now thrust at me with two blades. Like a young man he crouched before me, making brief passes in front of me with his knives, to keep me off centre. I crouched to echo his stance, but kept my blades, sword and knife, poised to strike, stone still as a hawk's head as she looks at her prey.

'Thorkil was weak,' Vasser said. 'Yet your mother preferred him. That Saxon trull. Like a filthy vixen she waited on him . . .'

I sprang at him. He caught me and pushed me back. I wrestled with him and he took my sword from me and threw it away. He held me with one arm under my chin, pressing the back of my head against his chest, as he let loose poisonous words.

'Fierce fighter, though. You have her fire. Even without weapons she almost did for me.' With what strength I had left I thrust myself away from him. Panting, I watched him as you would watch a venomous snake. 'Not strong enough, in the end.'

Vasser called to his warriors to stop the fight. With deep drawn breaths, they did so, and my force also lowered their weapons. They fell back to give us room. Vasser now sheathed his sword and we stood facing each other, each holding a knife, to finish it.

'I killed her, Beren,' he whispered. 'Thorkil suspected, but could not prove it. I did it. I killed them both.'

Rage filled me with one thought. To stab and stab, and stab again, until Vasser's flesh gaped with wounds. In a single move, I leapt for him and jabbed my knife up to his jaw, but he jerked his head away and the blow missed its aim. Off balance, I stumbled, and Vasser knocked the knife from my hand, put his fist in my hair, and dragged me upright, turning me round to show me to my warriors.

'Before I kill her, who will fight me for her life?' No one moved. Vasser kicked the back of my thighs until I fell to my knees. 'No one, it seems. You are without a friend.' He put his blade to my throat and jabbed lightly. It was not sharp, a mild sting only, but it grew warmer with each breath.

'Now I have you where you should be,' Vasser bent down to murmur in my ear. 'When you die, as you surely will—the venom on my blade is slow-acting but certain—they will not blame me. All saw you challenge me. You brought this upon yourself. Die, then, Berengeria. Though I'm truly sorry for it. You have your mother's eyes.

'I give her back to you!' he shouted. He let me go and I slumped forward, my face pressing on the cool ground. 'Wulf's queen has learned her lesson. There will be no more rebellion and no more talk of blood debts.'

Vasser was carefully wiping his knife. My fingers and feet were cold, but I couldn't move them to warm them, and a gradual darkness seeped in at the edge of my sight.

'Vasser Wulf!' Someone shouted from the top of the monastery fence. I blinked to see who it was and my bleared eyes fixed on one face among all, the face of one who, I saw, was about to claim a blood debt of his own.

From his vantage point atop the monastery fence, Cedd raised his bow, drew back his hand, then let loose a fatal dart. Above me, Vasser stood for a single breath, then fell back, the shaft of Cedd's dart sticking out of his neck. I gazed at Cedd and saw the face of my rescuer, the face of a friend.

CHAPTER 26
NEW BEGINNINGS

There was no more fighting, no fierce battle, no more slaughter. When Vasser died, his hearth-jarls sprang forward to encircle his body, holding out their swords to defend him, even in death. My own companions, Helga and Brand, lifted me up to speak to them. Standing, I managed to sheathe my own blade, as a sign to my force that the fight was over. Then with Helga supporting me, I went to the jarls. I couldn't speak—the sting in my neck throbbed with pain—but I pressed down their swords, one by one, with my outstretched hand, encouraging them to sheathe them. They did so.

Then Einar spoke to them and showed them their choices: either to ride out, free and unscathed, south to the war again, or to stay here, to join us and deliver the peace. Some left then, heading south, to join Guthrum, or, as I afterwards discovered, to cross the sea to raid in Francia and other lands.

Others chose to stay and were taken into the monastery, to have their wounds tended and their bellies filled. It was then that I lost my senses and was shamefully carried from the field.

I awoke, days later, with a fresh breeze blowing on to

my face from a windeye and Albi's face frowning down at me. His hand was touching my cheek. '*What . . . is . . . it?*' I hissed, like a toad, and he snatched his hand back and stuffed it into his sleeve as if it burnt. I tried to lift my head from the pillow and groaned. Father Anselm had bled Vasser's poison from my neck by making an incision which he afterwards stitched. I thought my throat was cut.

Grinning, Albi shook his head. 'Nothing's wrong. I'm pleased that you've recovered your senses,' he said.

When Winternight finally arrived, Asa held a celebration of sorts, in our old camp. We threw a little wine and wheat on our fire, giving thanks to the gods for our survival, but it seemed more of a leave-taking than a thanksgiving. The days after battle are a grey time, when the spirit seems old and thin, and no task fires the blood. So it was that Winternight. There had been deaths on both sides. Old friends, some of them Vasser's men, long known to us, had been killed. Thankfully, none of my small tribe was among them.

Still, the mood was dark, as we were forced to begin a new life here among the Saxons. Our old way of life was gone, the new way yet to reveal itself. We set up our sail roofs on the edge of the Saxon village. Brokk and Arn built their forge again. Sigrid set up her loom and showed the girls, Saxon and Viking, how to spin sheep's wool and what plants to gather for the dyes. Leif made rope again. Asa helped Skar with the hawks, and we took Cedd out hunting with them. Yet we wondered who we were.

Could we still call ourselves Viking? Men like Vasser had despoiled that name: perhaps that stain would never be washed clean. Some of us accepted it, and turned away from the old gods, towards the Christian. Perhaps Albi was right. Perhaps we had to give up our old ways. Still, it was a bitter thing, when, as a token of our good faith, Father Anselm asked us to give up our weapons to the common store.

Then one morning, winter finally showed itself and I woke up to first light glinting off fields swathed in hard frost, an armoured blanket covering the mess and ruin of our battlefield. As I took deep breaths of the cold air and felt it freshening my body, my blood stirred to a new beginning.

We had buried the bodies, including Vasser's, in a large pit, in top acre. Asa and Leif held the due rites, and we buried Viking and Saxon together, Christian and pagan. A Christian cross was put there to mark the site, though afterwards I saw that someone had carved a Viking warrior on one side of it, with his knife at his belt and his axe and his sword, to stand ward over the dead.

That day I passed there with Albi, as we rode out to take soundings of the land, to see what was needed before snowfall, what could be saved, what built up again, in the way of shelter and provisions. Anselm had further asked Albi to begin the task of allocating land to anyone who wanted to settle here and farm. The price was man-hours to be worked on the glebe land and the vow to take up arms with the fyrd, in defence of the settlement in time of war. Most of my people had accepted these terms and were looking forward to building their own home on their own land.

My own reward was a fine meadhall, to be built at winter end, out on the headland, beyond the monastery. I should have treasured this gift and welcomed it as a seal on the bargain of peace between us, but, as Albi and I rode out to examine the acreage, a fearworm writhed in my gut. It was a time of crossroads and new directions, of endings and beginnings, of continual throws of the die and anyone's guess as to which way it would fall. For Albi too.

'What will you do?' Albi said, knowing, as always, my thought before I could give it voice. I stayed silent, looking out at the grey rolling sea. 'Will you stay or go back to the Mark?'

'What will *you* do?' I asked.

At first Albi made no reply. Then he said, 'I'm going to Rome.'

'*Rome?*' I kept my voice low and gripped my reins with bloodless fingers, remembering Thorkil's words: '*Make a friend of the one who knows your name.*' What good was my friend if he went away, to the other end of the known world?

'Yes. There are scholars in Rome, men who will teach me.'

'When?' I said. From his dress and his pack, I already knew the answer. 'Beren—' Albi put his hand over mine. 'I have to go.' He pressed his fingers on mine. 'You could come with me. I want to learn all there is to learn, about the sea and the stars, about healing and music, about proper farming, about weapons, about other peoples and trade routes, about the new lands they think lie to the west. About everything.'

I pulled my hand sharply away. 'Not about how to make a peace and protect a people, about building roads and homes, farms and workshops and strong defences—'

Albi looked at the sea. 'That's your task.' In the silence that followed, I knew that he had to go, just as I had to stay. We had both made our choice.

'I'll be back,' Albi said. I moved away, clenching my jaw. *Why were the hot tears ready to spill over my cheeks?* 'To see how you're getting on with it,' he called. 'So you'd better be—getting on with it. No skulking and sulking inside this grand meadhall of yours—' I swung round as he gestured to the empty plot in front of us.

'Skulking?' I said.

Albi grinned and nodded, then tugged his rein and took off like the wind.

'*Sulking?*' I yelled after him and he threw up his hand and waggled his fingers at me.

Laughing, I caught up with him, by the river, and we dismounted and led our horses to water. As we stood together sharing our thoughts with the icy current, I drew my knife. Albi's eyes widened, until I handed the knife to him, hilt first, the gold fox head set into the horn handle, my father's sign, gleaming bright.

'Take it,' I said. 'Show it to the guards at the gate when you return. Our peace will be well-defended.'

Albi pushed the knife into his belt. Then he reached over and hugged me tight and when he let go, his face burned, as did mine.

'I'll be back,' he said, swinging himself up on to his horse, then without a second glance he took off across the ford and down the path to the coast, where, no doubt, his ship was waiting.

Sigrid saw him pass and called a greeting to me from the wood. Gerd was with her, helping to collect kindling. I waved to them, then mounted Snorri and set off back to the site of the meadhall, in need of time and space to think.

There I sat, not able to still my jangling thoughts, looking out over the grey northern sea, until I saw the small ship set sail, carrying Albi away on his great venture. Othinn keep him safe. And Gheez, too, I added, crossing myself as I had seen Albi do. Keep him safe.

When I could no longer see the tiny dot of his ship, I turned my back on the sea. Anselm had chosen the plot for the meadhall well. From here I could look out over the whole territory. To the monastery, where the gates stood open, for now, to everyone. To the marketplace, where we would trade with each other but also with travellers who passed along this great northern road. To the village where peaceful threads of smoke rose from fresh fires, where Asa and Helga, Brokk and Arn worked alongside Cedd and the other Saxons, to build shelters for everyone and keep the store barrels full.

To the fields where the farmers would till the land. To the woods, where we would hunt. To the river, which would carry us in our ships out to sea on adventures or deep inland, to explore there.

This was my land now. These were my people. All my people?

My mind began to settle and find clear direction. I would be queen, of a kind: a leader, a warrior, a protector, a provider, a peacekeeper. I would offer myself to their service. I would work with Father Anselm to deliver the peace. I would sound the advice of my peers, Einar and the jarls. Cedd and the Saxons. And, if they chose to stay at my hearth, they must accept joint moot. Jarl must deal with Saxon, Saxon with jarl.

It would happen. Here, we would make a peace. Whatever Aelfred Cyning and Guthrum decided in the south, here, for us, now, the long war was over.

PAULINE CHANDLER

Pauline Chandler was born in Nottinghamshire. After student years in London, she became a teacher and now teaches children with special needs. Pauline began to write seriously during a year's break in Cornwall. Her first short stories were published in local and national magazines. Besides writing, she enjoys gardens, wild woods, cats and architecture. Pauline lives with her family in a former Victorian gasworks in Derbyshire. *Viking Girl* is her second novel.

If you enjoyed Viking Girl, *you'll love* Warrior Girl, *also by Pauline Chandler.*
Here is a special extract, from the first chapter . . .

MARIANE

It was my grandmother who saved me. I was making everyone sick with my screams, the wordless noise that said *I want my mother! I want my mother!* They were all pleading with me to stop, but I couldn't help myself. Like a hog driven to slaughter, I bit and kicked and scratched. I stuck my foot in the door of my mother's room as they tried to push me away, dug my nails into the wood of the jambs until the ends of my fingers bled, all the time making animal grunts, my eyes forever fixed on the smudge of blood, that wrongness, at the side of my mother's mouth.

Through the closing gap of the doorway I saw my aunts arranging her body, one of them wiping the blood away, as my grandmother's arms closed on mine. Her arms are as strong as steel and brook no argument. So, as she prised me away, I gave in to her, let her lead me downstairs, let her sit me on her lap as if I were a baby again. And she held me so tight that, in the end, my rage vanished and I clung to her, because I knew she was saving my life.

My mother's murderers would have cut me down too if I'd run after them. And I would have, make no mistake; I would have dashed after them straight into hell itself, to kill or to be killed, but for my grandmother.

Even though I am grown, almost ready to marry and leave home, I submitted to the treatment: for hours she wrapped her shawl around me, and held me tight, rocking my heartache, singing. I think she expected, or, in the end, hoped, that it would bring back my voice.

Grandmère had a repertoire of songs which she sang to me during this time, always in the same order, one after the other, until I was soothed into sleep. My favourite was the first: '*Viens par le pré, ma belle*', 'Come into the meadow, my pretty girl'—as I sing it again, silently in my head, I can feel grandmère's warm breath on my face and hear again the soft sound of her voice as she murmured the words. The song is imprinted on my mind like a map to tell me who I am and where I've come from. One day, I'm going home, that's my plan: when the time's right, I'll go back there, I'll just go. Of course, Uncle Jacques will try to stop me.

I was sent here because it's too dangerous for me in Reims. Well, I shan't tell him: I'll wait until he's away or busy with the harvest or until I think he's forgotten my existence, then I'll grab my bag and I'll go home. I won't let grandmère send me back again.

They say it's a long dangerous road from Domrémy to Reims, but I'll travel at night, using the ditches and tracks that no one else uses. I'll stay off the road: the English are all over it like a rash. Even if I were seen, no one would bother with me. I'm a 'throwback', according to Uncle Jacques, a dimblebat, an idiot, because I can't speak. It makes me angry, but I don't let on. Underneath I'm stoking my rage, turning it into the energy I need to get back to Reims.

It's hot today, hot September. This field of turnips looks small from the farmhouse, but when you're in it and not even halfway through pulling the crop, it stretches out to infinity. To be honest, I couldn't care less if I never see another turnip in my life. I've been doing this job all week, with my cousin Jehanne. Which means, more or less, by myself, because as soon as Jehanne has filled her quota of baskets, which she does at top speed, she's off into Long Meadow. She lies down in the stubble, prostrate, like a nun in a church, making the sign of the cross with her body on the ground and she lies like that, quite silent, for hours. She says she is attending to God. She says she is listening for His message. This seems devout, but it can't be right, can it?

I hate turnips. They don't even taste nice. These are purple. Last week we pulled the yellow. The leaves are so hairy and rough, turnip-pulling ruins your hands. I wish my hands were like those of Father Cornelius: his hands are as soft as lamb's wool and his eyes are deep, like brown pools on a hot summer's day. I'd like my husband to look like Father Cornelius. He's slim and strong and his face goes quite still when he looks at you, which makes you feel special. The only thing is that sometimes a cold look comes in his eyes, as if he knows all your sins and has got you signed, sealed, judged, and sent to damnation.

He'd better not find out about Jehanne lying down in the fields. He'd probably think she was showing off and getting above her station; a mere woman trying to listen to God by herself instead of in church at the proper time. He wouldn't like that, I know he wouldn't. But if he asked me about her, I couldn't lie, so he'd better not.

She's getting to her feet. I shade my eyes to get a better view. She always knows when it's time for the bells to ring out the call to prayer and she stands facing the church, listening, as if the bells are ringing just for her.

'Mariane! Mariane!' It's Jehanne's mother, my aunt Isabeau. She's standing by the gate into the farmyard, tying a scarf round her hair. 'Where's Jehanne?'

Something's happened. She never fetches us from the fields, but she's hitched up her skirt and is treading over the ruts in the lane, crossing over to the gate. She stops and shades her eyes.

'Mariane!' I wave to show that I've heard, push floppy strands of damp hair back under my headscarf and rub the sweat from my brow, ready to pay attention. 'Where's Jehanne? I need you both back at the house.'

As if I've not heard the question, I wave again and walk down the field towards her, carrying two baskets of turnips, one in each hand.

'Where's Jehanne?' she says again.

As I get close to her, I stumble and spill my load at her feet. There are small dusty turnips rolling in every direction. Some end up in a stinking puddle, causing a cloud of shiny blue and green flies to explode into the air.

'Oh God—' she says, batting the flies away from her face, '—never mind—oh, dear—are you all right, Mariane—oh dear—never mind—' Automatically she helps me re-load the baskets, her mind obviously elsewhere.

'I'll take these,' she says finally, stowing the load under her arms. Then she says sharply, 'Fetch Jehanne. I need you both now.' As she turns away I hear her speaking to herself under her breath, as if organizing the tasks in her mind. 'We can use the dog-cart. One of them can pull it with a shoulder harness. Pray God it doesn't rain,' and then she's gone.

I climb back to where I can see Jahanne standing in the middle of the meadow, as still as a rock. Everything around her is still; the long grass, the poppies, the flax, stand as if in a painting. The insects are still and the birds. The trees look as if they're listening, or waiting, or both.

As I walk towards her I try not to make a sound, because I don't want to break the silence. Jehanne's silence. It's as if she can stop the world. I don't know how she does it, but I can feel it.

As I get close she turns slightly to look at me with that special smile of hers and the silence is broken and all the world moves again. I hear the hum of bees and the swish of the wind through the trees. As Jehanne steps forward to meet me a skylark rises from the ground at her feet. We both stop and tilt our heads, watching it soar high into the wide blue sky . . .